SAFE AS HOUSES

Simone van der Vlugt is one of Holland's bestselling crime writers. She has written eight thrillers to date, including *The Reunion* and *Shadow Sister*. The prize-winning *Safe as Houses* is the first to be published by Canongate. Simone van der Vlugt lives with her husband and two children in Alkmaar in the Netherlands.

SAFE AS HOUSES

Simone van der Vlugt

Translated from the Dutch by
MICHELE HUTCHISON

CANONGATE
Edinburgh · London

Published in Great Britain in 2013 by Canongate Books Ltd, 14 High
Street, Edinburgh EH1 1TE

www.canongate.tv

1

Originally published in 2012 in Dutch as *Blauw water* by Anthos,
Amsterdam

British Library Cataloguing-in-Publication Data
A catalogue record for this book is available on
request from the British Library

ISBN 978 1 78211 073 6

Typeset in Sabon by Palimpsest Book Production Ltd,
Falkirk, Stirlingshire

Printed and bound in Great Britain by
Clays Ltd, St Ives plc

SAFE AS HOUSES

1

She doesn't see the man until right at the last moment. Lisa is in the garden, hanging the washing on the rotary washing line, when all of a sudden he appears from behind the flapping sheets. She drops the sheet in her hands on to the grass with a yelp. The man looks so terrifying that she recoils, bumping into the table behind her. The washing basket tumbles to the ground, followed by the pegs.

The man studies her with squinted eyes. He looks quite scruffy, with crew-cut black hair and at least two days' worth of stubble. He is wearing worn-out cowboy boots, and his clothes are covered in grass stains, but it is mainly the icy look in his eyes that frightens Lisa.

A gust of wind makes the washing line spin, and the flapping laundry hides the man from view for a few seconds. Lisa seizes her chance and runs towards the kitchen door. The man steps around the washing line, beating aside the sheets that blow at him, and follows her. Just before she reaches the house, he breaks into a sprint. Lisa slams the door in his face, but before she can throw the bolt the man pushes it open and forces himself inside. His presence fills the entire kitchen.

Lisa's eyes race over to the knives hanging on the tiled wall above the worktop, but she knows she'd never be quick enough to reach them. She inches cautiously backwards towards the open door of the sitting room. The shrill sounds of the television programme her five-year-old daughter, Anouk, is watching on the sofa emerge from inside the room.

Lisa waits, motionless. The intruder does too, and they stare at each other for a length of time. Just as long as Anouk doesn't notice, just as long as she stays put, absorbed in her cartoon.

The man doesn't look particularly muscular, but he is very tall and Lisa knows that he could have her on the ground, no problem. She isn't going to fool herself into thinking that she could hold him off, though she can prevent him from catching sight of her daughter.

It occurs to her that he hasn't yet said a single word. She can't fathom him out – she has no idea who she's dealing with or what he wants from her.

As the man advances towards her, she retreats and holds on to the doorpost, but he heads towards the worktop. The remains of their lunch are there: the breadboard, half a loaf of brown bread, a packet of crackers and some chocolate sprinkles. Anouk's half-finished glass of milk is in the sink. She didn't want more than that today, and Lisa didn't want to force her. She probably would have spat it out again anyway.

The man grabs the glass and finishes the milk. Then he swipes the bread bag, ignores the knot Lisa has made in it and tears open the plastic. The slices come tumbling out, and the man stuffs one into his mouth without even considering the fillings on the worktop. He keeps one eye on Lisa as he eats.

She watches the scene in astonishment. The man is starving! Seeing him eat ravenously, she is in two minds. If she'd been alone, she could have run away by now. But she won't get far with Anouk. The best she can do is to try to make it clear to him that she's not his enemy, that she wants to help him.

She opens the fridge with trembling hands and reaches inside. As she does so, his large hand grabs her arm and his aggressive face looms very close, but when he sees that Lisa is holding a box of eggs he relaxes.

'I . . . I thought I'd fry you some eggs,' Lisa stammers. 'Would you like some?'

The anxious, submissive tone she hears in her own voice doesn't please her, but the man lets go of her arm.

Her legs feel as though they're about to disappear from under her, but she makes it to the worktop and opens a cupboard. As calmly as she can and without any sudden movements, she gets out a frying pan and sets to work.

Too close, he's standing too close to her. Lisa's hands clutch at the packet of butter. She'll have to slice off a pat, but she'd rather not draw his attention to a knife.

The butter is cold and hard, and she has to fiddle at it to remove the paper and squeeze off a chunk. She throws it into the frying pan and wipes her fingers on her jeans.

The butter hisses in the pan. Soon the eggs follow; she has broken them so clumsily she has to fish out pieces of eggshell. She is far too extravagant with the salt and pepper. It annoys her that she has lost control of her hands. At the same time she needs to keep herself busy and maintain the appearance of being calm.

She moves slowly and deliberately to the fridge, and this time he leaves her alone. Cheese and ham land haphazardly on top of the eggs, whose yolks are slowly congealing. The gas can be turned down now, and with a metal skimmer she lifts up the fried eggs from time to time. It feels good to be holding something she can use as a weapon, ill suited or not.

The man stares at the eggs. He inhales the cooking smell and then roughly pushes Lisa aside, grabbing the pan from the heat and dumping the ham and eggs on to the breadboard. He picks up the eggs and spreads them over two slices of bread, then he eats the meal standing.

Lisa watches him with her back pressed against the tiled wall. Hell, the man can eat. If he takes any bigger bites, he'll choke.

But the man manages to swallow every mouthful. When he's done, he lunges towards Lisa. She lets out a strangled cry, but he is only opening the fridge door to take out a carton of milk. He puts the opening to his mouth and swills down its contents, trickling milk over his unshaven chin and his clothes.

Lisa is suddenly breathless from the shock of it all. She leans back against the wall. What now? Will she be able to walk away and phone someone, or leave the house with Anouk? No, she has to avoid anything that might make him aggressive. Her house is just too far off the main road to take a risk. She would have attempted it on her own, but not with a sick child.

Her only chance is to make a call. Her mobile is on the dresser. All she has to do is to dial 112 for the emergency services.

Slowly she peels her back from the wall, but the man stations himself in front of her in an instant.

'Stay there.'

The command sounds very calm, which makes it all the more threatening. Lisa doesn't move.

The man throws the empty milk carton on to the worktop and looks through the open door into the sitting room. Anouk looks back at him from the sofa with frightened eyes. She is not keen on strangers. She is even shy with people she knows, if she hasn't seen them for a while. There have been times when she has stood in the hall for hours, not daring to enter the fray of a birthday party. Only when nobody is looking does Anouk creep in, and then her nervousness slowly but surely wears off.

Now she sits there in her purple Dora the Explorer pyjamas, staring at the strange man in the doorway. She gives her mother a panicky glance and her lip begins to wobble.

'Mummy?'

Lisa swiftly pushes herself past the man and places her body as a buffer between the uninvited guest and her daughter. If he wants to do anything to Anouk, he'll have to get past her first. It wouldn't be that difficult for him, but every second that she can keep him in the kitchen counts.

'Don't worry, darling,' she calls out reassuringly.

'Who is that?' the child asks fearfully.

'This man was very hungry. I made him something to eat.'

'But who is he?' Anouk repeats with the stubborn determination of a five-year-old.

The answer sticks in Lisa's throat. The man pushes her aside and lets his eyes travel around the open-plan dining-and-sitting room. It seems as though he is not sure what to do next.

Then his eyes rest on Lisa again and a look of calculation appears on his face.

'In there,' he says abruptly.

2

Deep in her heart she had hoped he would leave once his belly was full. Instead he is roaming around her house, picking up photos, opening drawers and looking in cupboards. She'll leave him to it: he can take everything in it, just so long as he leaves them alone.

'You have a lovely house.'

'Thanks.' It sounds stupid, as if he's an acquaintance paying a duty call rather than an intruder, but it's the only thing she can think of. Don't provoke him, whatever you do, don't provoke him. Wait calmly to see what his next move will be, and in the meantime keep standing between him and Anouk.

Thank God Anouk is sitting quietly on the sofa, her toy monkey clutched to her, as if she senses that it's best to remain as inconspicuous as possible.

'Nice stuff you have too.' His hand glides over an antique sideboard; he taps his nail on the edge of a crystal wine glass. Lisa shuffles backwards towards the kitchen and gestures discreetly to Anouk, but before she can slip off the sofa the man enters the sitting-room area.

He walks around the coffee table, his eyes fixed on the large colourful painting above the sofa. It's a piece Mark painted the year they first met, and it means more to Lisa than she can say.

'Art,' the man says, as though he were pointing out a flying saucer.

Should she say something or is it better to remain quiet? Not trusting her voice, she opts for the latter.

The man's gaze drops to Anouk. Unexpectedly he bends forward and holds out his hand to her. As Lisa rushes towards him, stumbling, Anouk begins to scream and kick her feet.

A wildness appears in the man's eyes. 'Stop it! Be quiet! Stop!'

Anouk begins to cry instead and runs towards her mother. Lisa tries to calm her with reassuring words, but she can't prevent her body shaking. If there's any chance to escape, this is it.

Keeping a careful watch on the man, she frees herself as gently as possible from the clasping arms of her daughter. And then she runs.

Pulling Anouk behind her, she runs into the

kitchen, then outside, into the garden. Just when she thinks they might stand a chance, she is grabbed by the hair and thrown to the ground. 'Run, Anouk, go next door to Aunty Rose!' she shouts.

Anouk stands a way off, hesitating. Their neighbour lives quite far away, and she is not normally allowed to go there. Her face is a giant question mark, full of confusion and unwillingness to leave her mother behind.

The man roughly drags Lisa back into the kitchen and stares at Anouk.

'Stay there!'

'Mummy!' Anouk's voice threatens tears.

'Run away, Anouk! Run as fast as you can!' Lisa shouts before disappearing into the kitchen.

The crunch of Anouk's feet running along the gravel path. For a second Lisa is relieved, then she sees the fist coming towards her face. The ceiling and the kitchen floor swap places in an explosion of pain. The kitchen floor is hard, but the feeling doesn't last for long. What follows is a soft darkness.

When Lisa comes to, she is lying on the sofa and she can hear the television news. A sobbing noise reaches her ears. 'Mummy, Mummy, wake up. Your nose is bleeding, Mummy.' Anouk gently wipes the blood from her mother's face with her pyjama sleeve.

There is no part of her face that doesn't hurt, but she is immediately alert. 'Where is he?' she whispers.

Anouk nods towards the kitchen. 'He's locked all the doors and windows,' she says, her voice shaking. 'And he's got out all the knives in the kitchen.'

'The ones from the wall?'

'And the ones we eat with.'

Lisa closes her eyes with a quiet groan. It seems like the bastard is preparing himself for a longer stay. They have to get out of here. But how to get out of a house in which all the doors and windows are locked?

Her eyes seek out those of her daughter. 'And upstairs? Has he been upstairs as well?'

'Everywhere. He was running around.'

It seems that he has made the most of the time she was unconscious. That's not a good sign. Where is the house phone? Its cradle is empty.

'Get my mobile. It's on the dresser,' she says quietly.

A small headshake from Anouk.

'He put it in his pocket. And the normal phone too.'

Defeated, Lisa sinks back down on to the sofa and racks her brains, trying to make use of the fact that he doesn't know she has come to and is able to make a fresh attempt to escape.

The garage. If they can get into the garage, they're safe. Her car is there, and the keys are in the ignition. The door to the garage is in the utility room, and it can't be locked: she lost the key ages ago and never went to the trouble of having the locks replaced. If the man leaves the kitchen, they can slip into the garage.

'Anouk,' she whispers.

Anouk's face immediately comes so close that their noses touch. 'Yes?' she whispers back.

'I'm going to pretend to be asleep so that he'll leave us alone. You mustn't let on that I'm awake, all right?'

'All right,' Anouk whispers.

'When he comes out of the kitchen, I want you to tell me, very quietly, OK?'

'OK.'

Lisa closes her eyes.

'Mummy?'

'Shh.'

Anouk stays sitting next to her mother, as quiet as a mouse, and Lisa can hardly control her emotions. Her sweet, big, little, brave daughter. What kind of a bastard do you have to be to do this to a child? Whatever else happens, she'll never allow him to do anything to Anouk, even if she has to scratch his eyes out.

Footsteps on the wooden floor. He's back. For a few seconds nothing. He's probably looking at her. She opens her eyes the tiniest of cracks but can make out only his shape. What kind of expression is he wearing? What is he going to do? Anouk's back against her stomach is familiar and warm, but it also brings out all her maternal instincts and an enormous sense of vulnerability. Then his footsteps move off, towards the dining area, the hall. She feels Anouk make a quarter-turn.

'Mummy, he's gone.'

In the hall the toilet door opens and shortly afterwards there's a clattering sound in the toilet bowl. Lisa sits up cautiously and puts her feet on the ground.

'Quick,' she says as quietly as she can.

3

There is no question of moving at speed. When Lisa tries to stand up, it is as if the walls around them are wobbling. Her hand reaches for Anouk's shoulder, and the child gives her a worried look.

'I'm all right again now. Come, quickly to the car.'

As quietly and as fast as they can, they tiptoe to the kitchen. The man flushes the toilet in the hall.

Lisa pulls her daughter by the hand through to the utility room and opens the door. It's dark in the garage, but they don't dare to switch on the light. A single gesture is enough to get Anouk into the car, and Lisa feels her way to the garage door. The heavy door begins to move with squeaks and scrapes, and after a further shove it slides open with a crash. Sunlight and fresh air stream in. Then a pair of boots appears in her field of vision, followed by a torn pair of jeans, and a hand holding a large knife.

It's only a few steps to her car. Lisa turns and runs to it. She pulls open the door, drops into her seat and sees in a single glance that the keys are no longer in the ignition. She jumps out of the car again, swearing. It is as though the presence of the man has filled up all the space and taken all the oxygen.

'Mummy!'

'Get out, out!' Lisa screams as she runs to the workbench at the back of the garage. She expects to be grabbed at any moment, but the only thing she hears is the scrape of the door as the garage is returned to the dark. In blind haste her fingers reach for the workbench. She finds a tool box and rummages around in it until she feels the heavy weight of a hammer. She spins around, looking for both the man and her daughter, but can see neither of them in the darkness.

'Anouk!'

All of a sudden the strip lighting comes on, blinking hesitantly and then resolutely bathing the garage in its violent glare. The man is on the left of the car; Anouk is in the backseat, sliding hurriedly across to the opposite side and tugging helplessly at the child lock.

Without wasting a second, Lisa opens the car

door and with the same fast energy holds the hammer aloft.

'Come near us and I'll batter you to death, I swear it!' she cries with a catch in her voice.

The man walks around and forces Anouk out and backwards, towards the darkest part of the garage, where they have no chance of escape.

Lisa darts in front of Anouk to protect her and swings . . .

'Drop it, bitch!' The man holds the knife poised and makes a stab at Lisa.

The hammer swings down and a scream suggests a hit, but when Lisa goes to attack again she feels a shooting pain in her hand. Warm fluid drenches the sleeve of her sweater before she realises in shock and disbelief that it is blood. The next moment a large hand clamps hold of her arm and twists it behind her back until she drops the hammer.

Before she knows it, Lisa is lying on the cold concrete floor and a knife is pressed against her throat. Behind her, she can hear Anouk calling, but Lisa finds herself remarkably calm. It occurs to her that she is no match for her attacker. With a weak child and a wounded hand, she is doubly handicapped, and if she continues to resist she'll be risking not only her own life but also Anouk's.

Her eyes seek out those of her attacker and she forces herself to keep looking at him.

'Please, don't,' she says with difficulty. 'I'll do what you want, but don't kill us.'

He hovers right over her, panting from the effort, an almost hysterical look in his eyes. The knife cuts into her skin.

'Please,' Lisa whispers. 'I'm sorry.'

'Shut it! Stand up!' The man pulls Lisa up and drags her out of the garage. Anouk runs behind them, like a nervous fawn that wants to stay close to its mother. Moaning in pain, Lisa allows herself to be shoved into the utility room, through the kitchen, and back to the sitting room, where she is thrown on to the sofa. Blood drips on to the wooden floor. The television is still on.

Anouk crawls up against her, and Lisa wraps her good arm around her. As if they've agreed on a strategy beforehand, neither looks up; they keep their eyes fixed on the trail of blood on the floor. The man plants himself in front of them with his hands on his hips. He stays like that for a time, watching them, until Anouk begins to sob. He sinks down on to the edge of the coffee table, the bloody knife still in his hand.

'Well,' he says calmly. 'Now we are going to agree on a few rules.'

At that moment the television programme is interrupted by a news bulletin.

4

ESCAPED CRIMINAL COMMITS MURDER

For the third time in recent months a dangerous criminal has escaped in the Netherlands. The man disappeared while on accompanied day-release from a psychiatric prison on Sunday afternoon.

The criminal in question is 43-year-old Mick Kreuger, who was convicted of several counts of murder just two years ago. The police have launched a nation-wide manhunt, but as yet they have no leads on the suspect's whereabouts. He is highly dangerous, having already taken one life in the course of his escape, and should not be approached by members of the public under any circumstances.

All three watch the announcement: Anouk with wide eyes that flick from the television screen to the man, Lisa with a dizzy feeling, Mick Kreuger tense with concentration. Lisa compares the image on the television to the intruder. This can't be real. This can't be happening to her, in her own home. Her breathing accelerates and her mouth becomes dry, but somehow she manages to keep a handle on her emotions.

Kreuger sits down on the sofa, and when the original programme resumes he zaps through the channels to other news coverage. On RTL4 there's an extra news piece about the murder victim, who was beaten around the head with a heavy object. According to a witness, the suspect fit Mick Kreuger's description.

The screen fills with the same photo of a tall, skinny man with black, shaven hair and dark eyes that peer out without a trace of emotion.

Lisa feels her limbs growing cold; the chill reaches her fingertips. Her hand throbs painfully and is still bleeding. She has taken off a sock to bind the wound, but she knows that what she really needs is a bandage. She presses her thumb and fingers to the wound to keep it as closed as possible and holds her arm up high.

In the meantime she tries to think. Now that she's sitting on the sofa as meek as a lamb, Mick Kreuger is paying little attention to her, and she wants to keep it that way.

She once saw a programme about armed attackers. The criminal psychologist who was interviewed advised viewers to just go along with everything if they were threatened. The attacker would be as tense and nervous as you were, and a cornered rat can behave unpredictably. If you aren't able to defend yourself, it's better to become passive and not make the situation any worse.

Lisa wonders if the criminal psychologist was speaking from personal experience or whether it was purely theoretical knowledge taken from one of her textbooks. Still, she could see the sense in it. She gives Kreuger a cautious glance. He's sitting on the other sofa, his body tense. Suddenly he jumps up and launches into a volley of swearing that causes Lisa to cringe.

Kreuger races around the room madly, holding the knife. Lisa doesn't know how she'd found the courage to try to escape. He would have cut their throats without a second thought. He might still do that. He's said so little all this time that it's strange – he's clearly not right in the head.

The best thing to do is to stay calm until help arrives. The man has escaped from a psychiatric hospital; he can't have disappeared without leaving some kind of trace. The police are bound turn up soon. Until then she must keep to her sole priority: to protect herself and Anouk.

She lays a hand on her daughter's forehead. She feels warm. Warmer than she was this morning. She could give her a puff on her Ventolin. But the inhaler is upstairs.

Kreuger is sitting on the edge of the sofa, staring ahead blankly. He taps the knife on the palm of his hand, tap, tap, tap.

A fit of coughing from Anouk breaks the silence, and Lisa touches her lightly on the back until it stops.

'What's up with her?' It's the first time Kreuger's spoken in a normal tone of voice, though his expression is still hostile.

'She's got asthmatic bronchitis,' Lisa says, trying to keep her voice even.

'Does she need medicine?'

'She could do with her inhaler, but it's upstairs.'

There's a silence as Kreuger observes her. 'Go and get it.'

Gratitude floods through her, and the relief is apparent in Lisa's voice as she turns to her daughter, 'Mummy's going to get your Ventolin. I'll be right back.'

Anouk gives Kreuger a suspicious glare.

'He won't hurt you,' Lisa says gently. 'I'll only be a second.'

Anouk's eyes beg her to stay, but a new fit of coughing takes over.

Lisa runs upstairs to Anouk's bedroom. There's a telephone extension here, but her intuition tells her that this is a test. If she takes the phone from its cradle, Kreuger might make Anouk pay the price. He's probably listening right now on the downstairs phone, waiting for the click to give her away.

She can't make a call; she can't even look for a weapon. There are plenty of things up here with which she could defend herself: scissors, a penknife, a loose floorboard with nails sticking out, any number of heavy objects. But as long as Kreuger is with Anouk, she can't take anything with her. Nor can she risk him giving her a body-search.

Lisa grabs the inhaler and the Ventolin canister from Anouk's bedside table. Her hand begins to bleed again from the exertion. She goes to get bandages, cotton wool and disinfectant from the medicine cabinet in the bathroom. When she turns around, Kreuger is standing there.

She represses a scream. Although he is slight, his height fills the doorframe. His presence makes the room feel small. She shuffles backwards but ends up flat against the wall.

Kreuger looks at all the stuff she's holding. 'What have you got there?'

'I need to bandage my hand. The bleeding won't stop.'

With a tilt of the head, Kreuger indicates that she should follow him and she obeys. He nods at the bedroom, and, after a slight hesitation, Lisa goes in.

'Sit down.'

There's no chair. He can only mean on the bed. Lisa awkwardly sits down on the edge. Kreuger lowers his long body next to hers. Close, far too close.

He takes her hand, throws the sock on the floor, rubs some disinfectant on the wound and places a sterile gauze on it. Next he applies a wad of cotton wool and begins to bind her hand. He must know what he's doing. Two minutes later her hand is professionally bandaged up.

'Thanks.' Lisa doesn't know where to look, hating the intimacy of the moment.

Kreuger doesn't respond. He stands up and Lisa automatically does the same.

They stand facing each other next to the double bed in which she spent so many passionate hours with Mark. Lisa breaks out in a sweat. As long as he doesn't . . . See, he's looking at the bed. And at her. She has to try to distract him.

'You must have done that before. Just like a doctor.' She holds up her bandaged hand.

'I did a first-aid course,' comes the gruff reply.

'Aha. Always handy.'

'It's absolutely necessary if you have children.

They could choke on a toy or fall into the water or cut themselves on something.'

Lisa nods in reply. So he has children. Children he feels such a responsibility towards that he has gone on a first-aid course.

'Mummy!' Anouk cries plaintively from downstairs.

Their eyes meet: Lisa's questioning, Kreuger's irritated.

Nevertheless, he nods at her, and she flashes him a quick smile to express her gratitude. This is how things are. She has to ask permission to go downstairs in her own house, and she has to be thankful for receiving it, she thinks as she walks down the stairs.

Kreuger's footsteps follow closely behind.

'I'm thirsty!' Anouk says weakly, as soon as they enter the sitting room.

'I'll get you some water. It's time for your medicine anyway.'

In the kitchen she holds a glass under the tap and pretends not to notice Kreuger watching her from the sitting room. She returns to Anouk and gives her a spoonful of antibiotic syrup, followed by the glass of water. Her daughter drinks and then Lisa holds the inhaler to her mouth. A single press on the button releases a stream of Ventolin into Anouk's airways.

Kreuger observes them without comment.

Suddenly Lisa feels more confident. If he'd been planning to murder them, surely he would have done so already.

Just when she is wondering what will happen next, the calm in the house is broken by the shrill sound of the doorbell.

5

She's been in denial for half an hour, but she can no longer repress the disquieting thought that she is lost. There's no point in just driving around like this any more. Senta sighs and opens the glove box to take out the road map. Not that she is expecting it to help her much, since she doesn't have a clue where she is. But perhaps she can work out where she went wrong and follow that road back.

Spread out, the map covers most of the dashboard and steering wheel. She studies it sceptically. She doesn't really need the map; she already has a suspicion of where she went wrong – at the roundabout, when she should have gone towards Appeltern. She probably got off one exit too soon. The sudden mist obscured the signposts, but she thought she knew which direction to take. The autumn weather is ridiculously changeable during this period, one moment wonderfully sunny, the next raining or misty.

Now she is stuck on a bumpy track heading towards God knows where. Senta turns on her headlights. The bright light barely cuts through the thick ribbons of mist.

Senta takes a deep breath. What now? Turn around and go back to the roundabout, or carry on in the hope of reaching a proper road? She opens the window and sticks her head outside. She looks around mistrustfully. Could she even manage to make a U-turn here? There could be ditches on either side for all she knows. She doesn't feel like getting out. God knows where she is. Just drive on, then. Even dirt tracks lead somewhere.

Senta continues with caution. The road surface becomes even worse: the wheels sink into deep troughs. Everything around her is grey and empty, as if she were approaching the end of the world. After five more minutes of lurching along, she hears a plaintive sound somewhere on her right, in the grey mist. It is a sheep bleating, and others slowly join in on the left and on the right.

Could she be driving through the middle of a field?

If that's the case, there's not much she can do about it. She carefully presses the accelerator and drives on. Tonight, once she's safely ensconced on the sofa at home, she'll be able to laugh about this adventure. Her three children will laugh about their mother, and Frank, with a tired glance at her, will make some comment about women drivers.

Maybe she'd be better off keeping it to herself.

Suddenly the wheels of her Peugeot get a better purchase on the road. The bumping stops; she's hit hard ground.

Senta opens her door. Looking down, she sees a stony surface, and when she peers in front of her she can make out the contours of a house in the distance. She's probably on private property now, but no one will blame her in this weather. At least she hopes not.

She follows the road, which goes past the house and climbs towards a canal. A little more gas and she's on the embankment, and when she reaches a fork in the road she puts on the brakes.

And now? Her intuition tells her to turn right, but she's already made the mistake of trusting her intuition. After a brief hesitation she decides to go back to the house she's just passed to ask for directions. In a moment of clarity she remembers to put on her hazards, then she gets out, locks the car and walks down the steep slope.

The house looks quiet and deserted. Ribbons of mist swirl around the sloping roof and engulf the flower pots and box trees in the front garden.

The gravel crunches under her feet as she advances towards the front door and rings the bell. An old-fashioned-sounding tinkle fills the space behind it.

No reply. The second time she rings she presses her ear to the door, but once the sound has died out there's nothing from inside. There is probably no one home, but it is difficult to tell through the frosted glass. To her right there is an extension with a garage door. She'll have to walk around the house. It's rather impolite, but the chance of getting even more lost puts paid to any thoughts of decorum.

Decisively, she starts on her way. There's a rotary washing line in the garden. The washing, a few shirts and a nightdress hang motionlessly in the mist. There's a sheet on the ground, surrounded by a jumble of pegs. The washing basket, which had probably been on the wrought-iron side table, lies on the grass a little further up.

It is as though someone is running chilly finger-tips along her spine. The thick mist, the doleful washing and the eerie silence around her cause her throat to tighten.

She casts a glance through the kitchen window. Nobody. Now she starts to feel a little afraid. She can hardly try the door or knock on the window-pane, can she?

This is stupid – she's going back. The embankment will probably lead to a village, no matter which way she turns on it.

She arches her neck and takes a step to the side to look in through the large windows of the sitting room. She jumps when she sees someone on the sofa. A young woman is staring right at her. Even at this distance, Senta can see how pale she looks and how unnatural and tense her posture is.

With a reassuring hand gesture and a smile, Senta tries to make it clear that she means no harm. The poor woman must have been terrified when Senta loomed up out of the mist. She raises her eyebrows questioningly and nods at the kitchen door, but the woman doesn't move. She is sitting next to a small girl, who is lying on the sofa under a duvet. The woman holds Senta's gaze for several seconds, then slowly raises her hand and brushes her blonde hair from her face. Then her eyes roam over to a spot in the corner of the room.

Something about her bearing sets off alarm bells in Senta's head. Maybe it is the fixed expression on the woman's face, or the bandage on her raised hand. A warning sign begins to flash. Don't take another step.

But she does. A small step – not towards the kitchen door but towards the window. The curtain obscures her view of the room, but the house has large windows on all sides, which must let in a lot of light in fine weather. Behind the sofa on which the woman sits there's another large window, and she can see the rest of the room reflected in it.

There's a man standing in the middle of the room. She sees a large knife in his right hand.

Senta automatically takes a step backwards. The man doesn't know that she's standing here; he probably assumes that she's still outside the front door. The woman is the only person who has seen her, but she doesn't make the mistake of letting her gaze travel outside again.

Very carefully, Senta retreats, relieved that she didn't knock on the kitchen door or, worse still, go inside.

She runs, her heart racing, back towards the front of the house. As she sets foot on the gravel path, she pulls up and forces herself to walk normally, like someone who has given up ringing the bell and is leaving.

She keeps expecting the man to come up behind her. She resists the temptation to look back over her shoulder and checks her pace all the way to her car. Only when she reaches it does she turn around. The house looks quiet, swallowed up in the mist again.

Senta gets into her car as fast as she can. She puts on her seatbelt and starts the engine. She hesitates for a second, mobile ready in her hand, but then she sees there is no signal. Get away – not a second to lose.

She presses the accelerator nervously, accidentally turns the wheel too far to the right and almost drives off the bank. With a frustrated curse, she corrects the manoeuvre.

She tears along the embankment. Ideally she'd go at it full throttle, but that would be too risky. She is already driving faster than she should be, and the curves of the road are looming up unexpectedly as it is.

Suddenly the mist seems to dissolve away. She can see quite a stretch of road in front of her and even the road markings. Senta speeds up immediately. There is no time to lose. She has no idea what was going on back there; perhaps that man was the woman's violent husband. But he could just as easily be an intruder. Whatever it is, that woman and that child need help.

She grabs the mobile phone from the seat next to her and dials 112. As it rings, she continues to drive. Usually she would have slowed down, but her foot on the accelerator seems to have a life of its own.

Suddenly she sees a bend in the roadside hurtling towards her out of nowhere. She frantically turns the wheel, swerving violently to the left. Her mobile falls and lands between her feet. Senta drags the wheel back to the right and goes to brake, but the telephone has become caught under the pedal. She desperately attempts to dislodge it with her other foot, as she tries to keep the wheel straight.

Too fast, she's going too fast! A new bend looms. The brakes screech but she knows she's not going to make it. The smell of burning rubber hits her; she can hear herself screaming as reeds smack into the bonnet. Then she has left the canal bank and is plunging down into a grey world in which light and water can no longer be told apart.

6

The first thing Senta realises is that she can't see any water, even though it must be there. Just a few seconds later there is an enormous splash, and her head hits the steering wheel. Her vision turns black, but the water around her ankles rouses her immediately. Dazed, she opens her eyes and feels her forehead. Lightning flashes of pain shoot across her retina and bore into her head.

The cold slowly rises up her legs. She sees water streaming in under the door.

At a stroke, the numbness disappears. The coming minutes play out before her – minutes during which she will fight under water with a door that won't open, gasp for air and drown.

She looks around in wild panic.

Outside the car, grey water ripples. Paralysed with fear, Senta seizes the steering wheel. Her body and soul become completely still. She sits motionlessly in her seat, as though the terrifying situation in which she finds herself can be held at arm's length.

Then the water splashes around her knees and the rising chill sends an enormous scream out of her mouth. She suddenly finds the energy to switch on the light in the car and to search for the buckle of her seatbelt with frantic hands.

Some people say you should wait until the car has filled with water, because then a large air bubble forms. This is nonsense. There isn't always an air bubble, and the stupidest thing you can do is to wait until the doors won't open any more and the electrical windows have stopped working. If you drive your car into water, you have around ten seconds until it disappears under the surface, ten seconds in which to open the windows, ten life-saving seconds in which to make your escape. With an emergency tool like a LifeHammer, you can cut through a seatbelt or break a window.

She doesn't have a LifeHammer.

In blind panic, Senta manages to unfasten her seatbelt; she grabs the door handle and tries to open it. It doesn't work. She hits the button that opens the window, but the electrics are out now, and the glass remains an impenetrable layer between her and the dark world outside. The headlights, which until now had projected broad beams of light through the grey water, extinguish.

The fastest escape route is through the side window, she knows. Windscreens are impossible to kick in. She turns around in her seat, leans her back against the door, places her feet against the passenger window and tries with all her might to push it out. The water pushes back. She simply can't kick hard enough; her high heels keep slipping away from the window. She wastes precious seconds kicking them off and trying again in just her stockinged feet.

The water is now gushing over the seats. Panting with fear, she kicks, stamps, batters the window with her feet. The glass is too strong.

Though she knows it is useless, she pushes the window button a few more times, but it doesn't help. Muddy water streams over her legs, rising to her chest. She batters away at the window and sobs. Her muscles become stiff with cold; her strength begins to ebb away.

It is remarkable the kind of knowledge that comes to you at moments like this. Drowning takes between three and five minutes, the first minute and a half spent still conscious. One and a half minutes – it doesn't sound long, until that moment comes ever closer and you realise that it means ninety seconds of burning lungs and pure death-struggle. Once you have gone through your oxygen reserves, blood stops flowing to your brain, and you lose consciousness within ten seconds – all facts she picked up from some stupid newspaper article.

Senta lies in the water, shaking. She pulls back her feet and sits upright. The car is sinking, the water coming in more and more quickly. It reaches her chin and she kneels to give herself a few seconds' respite. There is just one slight chance left. Her mind is clearer than ever before.

The moment arrives when her face hits the roof, and water streams over her eyes and nose, and she draws a final breath.

The car hits the bottom of the canal with a gentle thud. It is suddenly terrifyingly quiet and dark.

Senta feels for the door. The car is completely submerged and still, which means the pressure should have lightened enough for her to be able to open the door. She can hold her breath for quite a long time, but she knows her chances of survival are decreasing by the second. Her hand finds the door handle and pulls, as she pushes against the door with her shoulder. She seems to be moving the water; the door gives a little. With newfound energy she pushes a bit harder, but the effort causes her to exhale too much through her nose. Precious air is lost from her lungs. She feels her chest tighten, a throbbing in her throat.

Her need for oxygen becomes ever greater, but she represses the impulse to open her mouth. Her lungs scream for air. She bashes her entire body against the door in mortal fear. It opens slightly. She forces her arm through the gap and then pushes the door, as though through thick treacle, agonisingly slowly out of the way.

Something black suddenly appears next to her. She is grabbed and pulled from the car. A firm grip around her waist and up they go.

Progress is slow, much too slow. With her gaze fixed on a light spot above her head that seems to spiral on the surface, she works her way upwards. Her ears sing and a choking feeling nestles in her windpipe. Just a little further. Her rescuer swims with fast strokes, much faster than she could have managed. But she has no more oxygen in her lungs. All she has is that last gasp of air and ever larger black spots appear before her eyes.

Her rescuer almost lets her slip but he finds his grip again and pulls her upwards with him.

Her body becomes slack, giving up the fight. Just a few more seconds and she must open her mouth; she cannot prevent it. Her lips, which she has held tightly together all this time, begin to yield. She knows it is the beginning of the end, that within a few instants her lungs will fill with water.

She manages to keep her mouth closed for a

couple of seconds, then her mind screams from lack of oxygen and her head seems to explode.

Eyes wide open, Senta sees the watery surface above her head coming closer, but it's too late. Colours flash before her eyes – she sees stars and then her body is filled with a dark shaft. A release.

7

Thank God Kreuger hadn't seen that woman. The few seconds she'd stood there in full view on the patio seemed to last forever. Lisa had held up her hand to reduce the flow of blood and the pain, but also to show her wound to the woman.

Had she seen Kreuger? Had she seen the knife that he was threatening her with? Had the woman fully understood what was going on here? Perhaps – one moment she was there and the next she'd rushed away. This gives Lisa hope and enables her to better endure the pain in her face and hand. Hold out just a little longer – help is on the way.

A vague impression of Kreuger's voice telling her he won't harm her or Anouk pops into her mind. All he needs is a place he can hide for a while until the coast is clear. If they cooperate, nothing will happen to them.

Anouk leans against Lisa. From the moment that she saw her mother coming back downstairs with a carefully bandaged hand, she has seemed a little less afraid, and Lisa is happy for her to remain that way.

'What are you called, by the way?' Kreuger asks unexpectedly.

'I'm Lisa, and this is Anouk. She's five.' Her voice sounds a little hoarse, as though she is about to come down with flu.

'And she's ill,' Kreuger notes. 'Has she been ill for long?'

'A day or two.'

'And you called the school to tell them she'd be off for a while?'

Lisa nods.

'So they won't try to contact you for the time being?'

'No, but there's a chance a few of her friends might drop round.'

'You won't let them in.' It sounds like an order, and Lisa nods. What did he expect? That she'd let other children in?

'If anybody calls, you'll answer the phone and you'll behave normally. Don't hang up right away. Have a chat and do whatever is necessary to stop anyone finding out you have an unexpected visitor.' A grin spreads across his face as though he has made a particularly clever joke, and Lisa smiles dutifully.

'Whenever you're on the phone or people come to the door, I'll listen in and keep your daughter company,' Kreuger continues, and Lisa's smile slips from her face. He stares at her to check that she has understood. Lisa nods.

'How . . . how long will you stay here?' she asks in a faltering voice.

Kreuger's eyes glide over to the window and his gaze becomes hard. 'As long as I need to. Are you married?'

'Yes – my husband will be arriving home at half past five.'

It is not clear whether he has heard her answer. He continues to stare out of the window, and after a while he walks to the dresser, where around a dozen photographs are displayed in silver frames. More carefully than Lisa expects, he picks them up one by one and studies them for a long time. Photos of Anouk as a baby, but also faded photographs from her own childhood. Sunny snapshots of holiday destinations, of Mark and Lisa with their arms around each other, laughing and tanned. Memories of happy times, defiled by the hands of an intruder.

Lisa drops her eyes when Kreuger turns around to her. He walks over to the sofa with a couple of pictures in his hand and holds them in front of Anouk.

'That's you, isn't it?' His smile is friendly.

Anouk responds with a cautious nod, not entirely convinced that this is a man she wants to smile at.

'With your daddy?' Kreuger turns the frame over and studies the picture of Anouk, Lisa and Mark on a sailboat with interest.

'And with Mummy,' Anouk says.

'And where is Daddy now?'

Anouk looks in her direction for help. Lisa's blood freezes because she senses where these questions are leading.

'Well?' Kreuger insists. 'You must know where your daddy is? Is he at work?'

Anouk nods carefully without removing her eyes from her mother's.

'And what time does he usually come home?'

Silence.

'I asked you something!' Kreuger shouts and Anouk begins to cry in shock.

'He's gone,' Lisa says hurriedly. 'He lives somewhere else; we're separated.'

There is no point in beating about the bush; he'll find out anyway. There are no men's clothes in the house, and there is no shaving equipment in the bathroom. Apart from in the photos and in her heart, Mark hasn't left any traces at all.

Kreuger walks over to her and stops. She doesn't dare to look up at him.

'Just now you said your husband would be home at half five,' he says in a strange, low voice.

'I'm . . . I'm sorry. I thought you'd be gone by then. I . . .'

His arm moves quickly and his fist hits her nose. Blood spurts. Anouk begins to scream; Lisa cries out and puts a hand to her face. Then she puts her head between her knees and presses one of the sofa cushions against her nose in an attempt to stem the bleed.

'Look at me,' Kreuger commands in an icy voice.

Lisa looks up warily, her eyes filled with tears of pain.

'Don't lie to me again. I don't like lying bitches.' A threatening shine appears in Kreuger's eyes. 'If you do exactly what I say, nothing will happen to you. If you don't . . .'

'All right,' Lisa says in a stifled voice. 'I'll do what you say. Really, I promise.'

She means it. She doesn't know how long he's planning to stay, but however long it is, she'll manage. She doesn't have a choice; she'll just have to make the best of it. Win his trust, become his friend.

Does he mean that he isn't planning on doing anything to her? She has seen his face and she knows his name. Maybe he'll murder them once he's had enough of their company.

No, she says to herself. He's said he won't do anything and you'll have to trust that. You'll go mad otherwise.

It would take a lot to drive her crazy, but she still has to be careful not to lose her self-control. For Anouk's sake, but also for her own.

Slowly Lisa stretches out her arms and legs to relax the tense muscles. At the same time she concentrates on the task at hand: making friends with this mentally disturbed man who stabbed her hand with a knife and has twice given her a bloody nose. God knows what he's capable of – she's not going to try to find out. She forbids herself from thinking about it. She is able to do this: she can repress the anxious part of her personality and bring the other part forward. Deep inside her there is a switch that she can click with iron discipline, so that the shaking and stammering stop and her body begins to obey again.

From the sofa she can hear Anouk's squeaky breathing alternating with sobs. Lisa puts down the bloody cushion and turns to her daughter, but Anouk pushes her away.

'Mummy, your face is covered in blood,' she says with teary eyes.

'Shh, darling, don't cry. It looks worse than it

is,' Lisa whispers. 'Remember when you fell off your bike and you cut your forehead? That bled a lot too, didn't it? Even though it was just a little cut.'

'Is your nose still bleeding?' Kreuger asks in a businesslike manner.

Lisa carefully rubs a finger under her nostrils, looks at the result and shakes her head.

'Go and clean yourself up in the kitchen.'

She gets up carefully. 'Anouk, Mummy's going to wash away the blood. I'll be right back – you'll see that it's fine.'

Sitting up stiffly, Anouk follows her mother to the kitchen with her eyes.

Strange, she doesn't know where the wipes are any more. Stunned, Lisa stands in the middle of the kitchen. It costs her some effort to remember. Of course, in the utility room. She reaches in the cupboard for a clean cloth and holds it under the cold tap. She carefully cleans away the blood.

From time to time, she looks out of the kitchen door at the back garden and the field stretching out beyond. The mist has lifted. The dirt track to the nearest village is quiet and empty.

8

Lisa used to think that happiness was something you could demand, like a kind of birthright. If you had a positive attitude, life couldn't really hurt you. Being happy was a character trait, she thought, and deep in her heart she harboured a quiet scorn for people who complained about their lot or sank into depression. If they'd only fight against it instead of wallowing in their misfortune, she'd have a lot more respect for them.

Nowadays she knows that happiness doesn't depend on your attitude, and you certainly can't force it. She has never stopped being positive, but she is now much more aware that people are fortune's playthings. And some people really get tossed around.

She no longer confuses real life with the romantic imaginings she used to have. She knows that you can be struck down unexpectedly by adversity, and she feels she's had her fair share with Mark. But here she is now, in a situation she never would have imagined possible and in which she is completely powerless. Held hostage in her own home. What are the statistical chances of an escaped criminal choosing your home as a hideout? There's more chance you'll win the lottery.

Why me? she thinks, but the answer is quick to follow: why not? The nutter might just as well have forced his way into Rosa's house a bit further along, but he didn't, and Rosa has no idea that she should be counting her blessings.

Lisa spends the rest of the day on the sofa with Anouk. She reads her daughter's favourite books out loud to her, while discreetly keeping an eye on Kreuger. One moment he is sitting in front of the television zapping away and the next he has jumped up and is pacing restlessly through the house.

He's right to be nervous, Lisa thinks with grim satisfaction. It can't be long before the police arrive.

She can't understand where they've got to. That they've lost Kreuger after his escape is one thing, but the woman who was here this afternoon and looking in through the window must have reported him. Don't they believe her? Or is she one of those people who would rather not get involved and has just gone home?

No, Lisa thinks decisively. She wouldn't do that. If she herself had had the slightest doubt about whether something was suspicious, she'd have done something about it.

But the same isn't true of everyone, says a voice worrying away inside her head. In this violent, selfish world, there is only one lesson to be learned: it's better to look away from problems if you don't want to be blamed for another funeral.

'Don't stop reading, Mummy.' Anouk looks at her with drowsy, feverish eyes and Lisa continues mechanically with the story. She hadn't even noticed she'd stopped. When she finishes, Anouk closes her tired eyes.

'Good girl. Have a little sleep.' She strokes her daughter's soft, dark hair tenderly. When Anouk coughs, she hears the phlegm rattle in her lungs.

'Seems like all the kids have got asthmatic bronchitis these days,' Kreuger growls.

'It's getting a lot more common.'

'That's because of the bloody pollution. We're poisoning the world and our children are paying with their health.'

Could Kreuger's own son or daughter have the same illness? Before she has time to think, Lisa has asked him. Kreuger slowly turns towards her. For a moment she worries that she's ruined the relaxed atmosphere, but Kreuger simply answers.

'Yes, my son had bad asthma. Much worse than hers.' His remark is accompanied by a surly glance at Anouk, as if it's her fault.

'Do you think it was because of the pollution?' Lisa asks cautiously, more than aware that Kreuger had spoken in the past tense.

'Yes, of course it was the pollution. We always gave our children healthy food, but we lived in the middle of a city. Every morning they had to cycle to school through heavy traffic and exhaust fumes. We should never have stayed in the city.' Kreuger stares ahead, to a past that Lisa is unaware of, but that she is keen to learn more about.

His breathing quickens and his eyes dart around restlessly.

'They say that the temperature of the earth is rising because of the carbon-dioxide emissions in the air,' she says to distract him. 'CO_2 is an insulator, so that fits. But it seems that there's not as much CO_2 emitted as we think. With everything that people have burned and produced in terms of exhaust fumes, the earth has only been warmed up very slightly. For Al Gore's doomsday scenario to happen, we'd need to emit three times more CO_2, maybe more.'

As she talks, she keeps an eye on Kreuger. He doesn't seem to be listening, but she continues all the same.

'It's debatable whether people have caused the greenhouse effect. Volcanic eruptions release CO_2 into the air, and in the billions of years the earth has existed the temperature has always gone up and down.'

'Really?' Kreuger asks with a complete lack of interest.

'Yes – they found that out by drilling into the Antarctic ice. The deeper you bore, the older the ice that you bring to the surface. They discovered from the composition of the ice that there is a link between the temperature and the CO_2 concentration at the time. During the time of the dinosaurs, for example, CO_2 levels were ten times higher than now, but it wasn't ten times warmer. Actually it was the other way round: thousands of years after the temperature rose, the CO_2 level went down.'

Kreuger looks her up and down. 'What a clever clogs you are,' he sneers. Lisa mumbles that she just read it somewhere.

Kreuger turns away with a snort of derision. 'Women . . .' he says. 'Tell me something about your husband. Where is he and why did you break up?'

It is clear he wants to know whether they are still in touch – and whether Mark might turn up unexpectedly. Lisa thinks quickly.

'Mark and I got divorced because he was horribly

jealous,' Lisa says with a strange remoteness in her voice, as though talking to herself, not to a total stranger who couldn't give a damn. 'His jealousy was a kind of illness, and it drove me mad. At the beginning of the relationship I found it endearing, flattering even. But that changed when he began to spy on my every move.'

For the first time Kreuger's face expresses interest. 'What did he do then?'

'He checked up on me, called me the whole time to ask what I was doing, who I was with and what time I'd be home. At first I used to tease him about it, but one evening he was furious because I came home ten minutes later than I'd said I would. He was convinced I was hiding something.'

'And were you?'

'No, of course not. I loved my husband.' And that's still true – at least, the man he once was.

Something flashes in Kreuger's eyes. 'All women cheat. They're whores.'

'I didn't. I loved my husband – he was all I needed.'

The left side of Kreuger's mouth twitches: the beginning of a smile, which then collapses. 'All women are whores,' he repeats. 'It's in them – maybe they can't even help it. It's in their genes: flirting, challenging, seducing, lying, fucking other men.'

Don't react, don't move a muscle, don't contra-
dict or agree. If she can't figure out the best thing
to say, she's better off keeping silent.

She casts a swift look in Kreuger's direction. He
is sitting on the arm of the sofa and cleaning the
dirt from under his thumbnail with the knife.

'Whores, the lot,' he mutters.

Then there's a silence that hangs heavily in the
room. There is something provocative and scornful
in Kreuger's expression, as though he is challenging
her to continue the conversation while knowing
that she doesn't dare.

'Are you married?' she asks casually.

For a moment she's scared she has gone too far.
But to her amazement he continues to pick at his
thumbnail and shrugs.

'I'm not divorced, so you could say I'm married,'
he says. 'My wife is dead.'

He checks for her reaction, and Lisa knows she
should hold his gaze.

'I'm sorry,' she says, as sincerely as she can
manage.

'I'm not,' he says indifferently. 'She was a whore.
I had to kill her.'

9

The first thing she becomes conscious of is the sterile air she's breathing. Around her she can smell cleaning products and a trace of alcohol. Then she realises that she has no idea where she is.

It's completely dark. A darkness so absolute that there isn't even a hint of grey anywhere. Whatever she is lying on is soft and warm like a bed. It *is* a bed. Her own bed?

She tries to picture her bedroom, and sees a space with a whitewashed wooden floor, freshly decorated with apple-green curtains and yellow bedding. The way the light falls, the smell, the things that complete the picture, are absent, telling her she's not in that room.

She wants to turn her head to try to see her surroundings but it's difficult. Worse, it's impossible. And why can't she see anything? It can't be that dark; even in the middle of the night you can usually make out something. Here she can't even work out where the door is.

Alarm washes over her. She tries to breathe evenly, but her growing fear is difficult to repress. When she opens her mouth to call out, her throat releases no sound.

Fear shoots through her. Opening her eyes wide, she stares into the intense darkness and wonders where in God's name she could be.

A voice reaches her from far away. It doesn't sound familiar and she can't make out all the words, but it is the only purchase she has in the darkness spinning around her. A man's voice, gentle and reassuring.

All her senses focus on the voice. Someone must have turned on a light in the far distance, because behind her eyes there is a grey haze in which shadows are moving.

'Where am I?' she asks, but her mouth won't move.

The voice is speaking to her, but the words enter her mind as gibberish. She listens to the sounds that softly lap against her like waves. It is reassuring that someone is next to her. In any case she is not alone.

Then she feels herself sinking away, more and more quickly, into a heavy, syrupy darkness, like a freefall into outer space.

Time passes but she doesn't know how much. Moments of inky darkness and a more diffuse world are separated from each other by a paper-thin haze. She often sleeps, if you could call it that, and when she floats to the surface she lies there, keeping vigil with her eyes shut. Her body remains motionless, but thoughts and images race through her mind.

Something changes. From time to time there is a bright light near her eyes, though she still can't see at all. She hears voices more often around her, and then she catches words that are familiar. She understands that they are talking about her and comes to the conclusion that she is in hospital. At once the proof of this becomes apparent. The beeping of the machines around her, the routine movements when her body is unexpectedly picked up and rolled over.

She is washed, and they speak to her in a friendly babble, the kind you use for the elderly and the infirm. Though she tries her hardest to understand what is being said, she picks up only fragments.

'. . . slept well . . .' '. . . have a look . . .' '. . . going again . . .'

In one way or another, she has ended up in hospital. She has no idea how or why, but that will come. She can still think and draw conclusions. Her memory might be temporarily absent, but there is nothing wrong with her thought processes.

But she is clearly not well. If she tries to concentrate on her surroundings for any period of time, her spirit gives up and falls away into no-man's-land, no matter how hard she resists.

It would be easy just to float around in the soft, shadowy world around her. The darkness has withdrawn a little and is reluctantly making way for a little colour. Blue, a gentle blue, like the ocean on a sunny day. It is pleasant and relaxing here, but the calm repose of her existence is regularly interrupted by an unwelcome flash of light, like the lightning before a thunderclap. She cringes inside because she knows what comes next: a bright, all-consuming headache.

But afterwards her head feels clearer and more tidy, as though there has been a great clear-out, creating space for the shards of memory that slowly rise to the surface.

10

Above the surface of the water, two shapes look down at her. She reaches out her hand but the rescuer's grip on her wrist does not come.

The voices talk on. The sound is distorted, but she can still understand. Not fragments but complete sentences, and the meaning is completely clear. She is in a coma. This is a shock, though no surprise. Whoever she is and whatever has happened, one thing is certain: she has to wake up. A person waking up gets up, pushes themselves up. She is not capable of it physically, but spiritually she can. Each time unconsciousness threatens to drag her back down, she resists with all her might. She focuses her inner eye upwards and strains as hard as she can, like a drowning man floating on his back, pushing his belly upwards.

Waking up is a serious test of strength. It's like being at the gym. Only she has never been so exhausted. Finally she has to give up and return to her gentle, heavy repose.

It is dark around her. How long has she been away? She can't allow herself to keep slipping back under water. That she has no control over her return isn't good. She will have to focus on the surface above her head, break through like a swimmer gathering all her strength to try for a gold medal.

Life is up there waiting for her, whatever kind of life it may be. It can't have been that bad if she is so desperate to get back. She swims forward using all her willpower, but a cold undercurrent tugs at her. She just manages to stay afloat in the blue water and not sink down to the darker depths. The blue water offers hope, she realises intuitively. The more often she is dragged into the depths and the longer she stays there, the less chance she has of ever breaking through to the water's surface.

She is suddenly overwhelmed by a feeling of loss and loneliness.

'Frank . . .' she whispers, but under water the sound of her voice dissolves as soon as she speaks the word. Frank?

The only thing to do is to swim around and wait until somebody comes. People have sat by her bed – their voices sounded familiar, but they didn't manage to pull her to the surface. Before she knew it, she was tumbling back down into the black depths, and when she came up again she was alone.

Now she lies on her back and waits. It is taking a long time. Perhaps she should let herself sink into the deep darkness – it might be better than lying here trapped in a body upon which she cannot impose her will. She rejects the thought immediately: of course it's better to be aware of herself and her environment. Intuitively she knows that every time she takes a freefall, she moves one step closer to death. It is essential to stimulate her mind, to remain active, so that she can wake up properly.

A face suddenly flashes through her mind's eye. A handsome, tanned male face, framed by messy dark hair. He smiles at her and she feels her heart go out to him. She loves this man, but as well as love she feels intense pain. She feels like crying, but her body doesn't obey her command, so she buries the feeling of sorrow and tries to extract some more information from her mind.

Just as she is about to remember something, she is dragged down again. Deep under the water she swims around, trying to find an exit route. But the inky darkness holds her prisoner.

The next thing she becomes aware of is the squeaking of wheels that definitely need oiling. She is being moved; her bed is being pushed along. A young-sounding female voice is telling her that they are going for a scan.

'You can hear us, can't you? I think you can hear us,' she says. 'It feels like something has changed. Look, your eyelids are fluttering again! Are you trying to tell me something? Try again?'

Her eyelids flutter; she blinks, opens her eyes wide and blinks several times more. Above her, there is a disappointed sigh. 'Well, perhaps it's asking too much. Let's look at your brain first. Good luck, sweetheart.'

She is rolled into a room where her body is lifted by several hands and pushed into something. The voices around her fall silent and a loud buzzing fills her head. Slowly she sinks away. When she becomes aware of her surroundings again, she is back in her own room.

There is a visitor.

'Where has she been?' A stool is shifted next to her bed, and a male voice speaks with a nurse. It is a familiar voice, but she can't attach a face or a name to it.

'We've been on a little trip,' the nurse says. 'We did an MRI scan.'

'But you'd already done one, hadn't you?'

'Yes, but we have reason to believe she's in the process of waking up, so the doctors wanted to see if there was increased brain activity.'

'And?'

'We haven't had the results yet, sir.'

Brisk footsteps on lino – the nurse is walking away. The stool's legs scrape on the floor as it is moved closer to the bed.

Warm lips gently brush her forehead. 'Hello, darling.'

It must be someone she knows really well. Perhaps her boyfriend or husband. Is she married? In any case, there are people worrying about her, which is a comforting thought.

The man is sitting on the right-hand side of her bed; suddenly she hears another voice on the left. The light, young voice of a child, a young boy, followed by another, that of a girl. They are talking to each other, and now and then to her, but she is too tired to concentrate on the meaning of their words. They put earplugs in her ears and she hears music. She feels them holding her hands, the boy her right one and the girl her left, and she hears the word 'squeeze'. She understands what she is supposed to do, but doesn't have the strength to do it.

'Mummy,' the girl's voice says tremulously. 'Mummy, can you hear me?'

Mummy? So she's a mother and she has a daughter. And a son too. Oh God, she can't remember any of this. What is she going to do when she wakes up? And what if she never wakes up and has to float around in this void for ever?

'If you can hear me, squeeze my hand, OK? If I feel anything at all, it'll be enough.'

'Yes!' she screams at her daughter. 'I can hear you! I can hear you!'

The girl takes her hand and intertwines their fingers.

She squeezes as hard as she can, enough to give her daughter a bruise, surely. She waits for her reaction.

'Senta?' The male voice sounds tense.

Her entire body is frozen in shock, completely rigid.

Senta.

At the sound of her name, she is suddenly allowed a glimpse into her memory. Something clicks inside her head, and her brain whirrs into motion. It produces a slow stream of information that she tries to piece together, joining the parts like the pieces of a jigsaw puzzle. She is called Senta, she is forty-three, married to Frank, the mother of three children. This morning, if it is in fact the same day, she left home early to get to Oss; she is a journalist and was making her way home from there. One at a time, the details of that morning come back to her, and she feels a warm wave of relief. If her memory is coming back, her body will start to work again too.

She tries to see what else she can remember, because she's now sure that something must have happened on the way home. The first thing that occurs to her is the mist. That treacherous, fast-rising mist that suddenly floated up around the car and obscured her view of the road. Did she have an accident? She can't remember; there are no more images. The last thing she can remember is attempting to read the signs at a crossroads. As she thinks back, she gets a flash of herself cursing and swearing from pothole to pothole on a barely navigable road.

Think again – it'll come back, she tells herself. If you try hard enough.

But nothing else comes. The mist, the crossroads and the bumpy road – this is all her memory will give up.

She turns to her family then, the names of her children. What kind of a mother is she, if she can't remember her children's names?

The girl's voice has released a flood of emotion that she can translate only as motherly love. Even if she cannot remember her daughter, the sound of her voice is enough to trouble her heart. Her lovely, unconfident, rebellious, adolescent daughter.

Denise.

Out of nowhere and without any effort, her memory has given her back her children: Denise, Jelmer and Niels.

Meanwhile she finds herself overwhelmed by an immense loneliness, a howling need to return to the world in which she belongs.

Senta looks up desperately at the surface, suspended like a tough membrane above her head. A whole life is waiting for her, a rich life full of promise. She has to wake up, wake up, wake up, wake up.

11

Pasta sauce. Herbs. Spaghetti. Garlic. Tomato and onions. All laid out on the worktop in front of Lisa, as though it's a normal Monday. The weather forecast had been good: it had been a lovely, warm, late-summer's day. September is warm this year, almost muggy. The trees have begun to change colour, and spiders weave delicate webs in front of the windows, but the sun shines on imperturbably, as though the time to take things down a notch hasn't yet arrived. When this afternoon's mist had closed in suddenly, it was a surprise. It has lifted now, but the sky is still grey.

Lisa tries not to look at the bandage she has just changed. She was shocked by the wound. It didn't look good, with its open flesh and dark edges. Though that doesn't necessarily mean it's serious. The bleeding has stopped, but the pain has not lessened. Despite the paracetamol, the wound continues to throb.

The extractor fan hums, sucking away the pervasive smell of onions and garlic.

Spaghetti is Anouk's favourite food, and Lisa had decided earlier that they'd have it for dinner. It was a way of making sure that Anouk would eat at least a few spoonfuls. Now she wonders how much she'll be able to get down herself.

The smell of fresh herbs and the delicious juice from the tomatoes on the chopping board do their best to tempt her, but she knows she'll have to force herself to eat. It's important that she eats to keep up her strength. You never know when you might suddenly need it.

From time to time, she checks on Anouk. To her alarm, Kreuger is sitting next to her on the sofa, talking quietly. Anouk is nodding and shaking her head, but not saying a word. Lisa longs to listen in on what Kreuger is telling her; but, whatever it is, Anouk is fending him off, and she pulls up her knees to make a barrier between them.

Has Anouk realised that she should keep on this man's good side, not repel him? Anouk has seen too much to give this uninvited guest the benefit of the doubt. Luckily, she is intuitive, like most children, and seems to know how to behave. She has limited herself to nodding and headshaking so as not to say the wrong thing, and she's even stopped herself from making the mistake of whining or crying. Instead, she is keeping a keen eye on Lisa and copying her behaviour: a calm, distant, wait-and-see attitude.

With as much composure as she can muster, Lisa goes into the sitting room and sets the dining table. Three placemats, three plates, just like it used to be.

Back in the kitchen, she gathers up the cutlery. Just a fork and spoon – the absence of knives isn't a problem with spaghetti. As she puts the cutlery next to the plates and a trivet for the pan on the table, she strains to overhear something of the conversation Kreuger is having with her daughter.

'You probably think I'm a really nasty man, don't you?' she hears him ask.

Silence.

'Answer me now,' Kreuger insists.

Anouk's eyes find her mother's.

Answer him, Lisa wills her.

Anouk takes a deep breath. 'Yes. You hurt Mummy. And Mummy didn't do anything wrong.'

Her voice sounds as accusing as a five-year-old's can be.

Kreuger slowly holds out his hand to her, and Anouk recoils just as slowly. Every muscle in Lisa's body tenses, like a predatory animal preparing to spring to protect her young.

Kreuger touches Anouk's cheek gently, as though she might crumble at the slightest touch. He lightly strokes her skin with his thumb.

Anouk's face darkens, as though she doesn't know whether to cry or to bite Kreuger's hand.

'Mummy didn't do what I said,' Kreuger says in a gentle voice. 'And you didn't either, but you can't help that. The next time you don't listen to me, though, I'll be even less nice. Do you understand?' His hand moves to her chin and lifts it up. 'Do you understand me, Anouk?'

'Yes, she understands. We both do,' Lisa butts in quickly.

Kreuger swings around. 'Shut your mouth!' he screams at her. 'I was talking to your daughter, not you!'

Lisa takes a terrified step backwards. 'All right, all right. I'm sorry.'

After a few seconds Kreuger calms down again. 'If you both do exactly as I say, nothing will happen to you. Then I'll be off and you can act like nothing ever happened.'

You pathetic bastard, Lisa thinks. You hold us hostage, you frighten my daughter; she'll have nightmares for years now. And if she doesn't, I will.

With a superhuman effort, she manages to smile and nod. 'Fine, agreed. Well, I'll finish off the dinner, then. It's almost ready.'

'This is nice,' Kreuger says.

They're sitting at the table, Kreuger facing them. He is eating with gusto but in a refined manner, not like the savage who forced his way into her kitchen. He must have been a civilised person once, a father and husband, an employee, someone's neighbour in a row of terraced houses in a respectable street. A man who taught his children table manners and complimented his wife on her culinary skills. An attentive and caring man.

They eat without any conversation. The television, which Kreuger wants to keep on all the time, breaks the silence. This, and the sound of their forks and spoons as they twist their spaghetti. Anouk looks a little better: the fever has gone down, and she is actually eating something.

It is still light outside, Lisa notices, but not for long. The darkness falls more quickly each day. It doesn't seem so long ago that they could eat outside and sit on the terrace enjoying the sun for a while afterwards. Yet it still feels warm and summery during the day: yesterday she'd put on a vest and shorts and done some work in the garden.

She keeps looking over Kreuger's shoulder at the

borders in the garden, the blooms of hydrangeas, pink phlox, hollyhocks and salvias fading with the light. Plants that she put in herself when she moved here and that she cherishes; their beauty fills her with happiness each year. She loves September, especially when there's an Indian summer. But now she wonders whether this autumn might be both her loveliest and her last.

She doesn't dare count on Kreuger's promise that nothing will happen to them if they play along. How much can you trust a criminal sentenced to psychiatric incarceration? He is calm now and doesn't look that dangerous; she has to keep it that way. It's still possible that the police might come, but deep inside doubt nags away at her. They should have been here ages ago. How much time does it take to write up a report and investigate the given address? Even if the police didn't take the woman seriously and weren't in any hurry, at least one policeman should have knocked on her door by now.

She cannot imagine that the police would be so lax as to do nothing. The only possible conclusion she can reach is that the woman didn't report it. Maybe she didn't even see Kreuger standing there; and, if that's the case, she would have misread the situation.

Kreuger serves up seconds. At least he's enjoying

71

dinner. Her dinner – her plate, her fork and spoon, her food. Sitting in Mark's place. As if he's planning on staying for good.

Lisa sips from her glass of water, but she has difficulty in swallowing. The despair flooding through her is suddenly so immense she has to do her best not to burst into tears.

Why has she been fooling herself? The woman hasn't gone to the police, and no one is coming. She's completely on her own.

12

Of course she has thought about the coming night. Several times the question of who is going to sleep where, and how, has shot through her mind. Lisa doesn't think there's much chance of Kreuger letting them sleep in their own beds, but she has managed to repress the thought for the entire afternoon.

But now that dusk is creeping around the house, nestling into the far corners of the garden, and the sky has taken on a dark blue tint, Lisa knows it is time for the second act.

They have eaten; she has tidied everything away and put the plates in the dishwasher. Anouk is playing a game on the computer at the workstation. Kreuger is sitting on the edge of the sofa, watching TV, tensely leaning forward. He zaps until he gets to the seven-thirty news on RTL4.

The news starts with Kreuger himself. Lisa catches fragments of the coverage from the kitchen and stands as close as she dares to the open door.

'There is still no sign of the escaped psychiatric criminal Mick Kreuger . . .'

'If he doesn't take his medicine, he may become dangerous . . .'

'It is believed a man was killed by Kreuger in the course of his escape . . .'

'Kreuger was sent to a psychiatric prison two years ago for the murder of . . .'

Lisa rushes back to the worktop and tries to marshal her thoughts. What will happen if Kreuger has to go without his medication for any length of time? All his murderous instincts, usually repressed by the drugs, will surface.

Her hand rubs her painfully throbbing temples, and she takes a sip of water to wet her dry throat.

When she turns around, Kreuger is suddenly in front of her. Lisa catches her breath sharply.

'I fancy some coffee,' is all Kreuger says.

'I'll put some on.' She turns to the espresso machine and switches it on. The machine comes to life with a splutter.

'Did you hear that?' Kreuger asks, nodding towards the TV.

'I was busy. The television is just too far away. Why? Were you on the news?' She manages to keep her voice light, as though it's totally normal for Kreuger to be on TV. It's quiet behind her for so long that she regrets asking the question. Kreuger comes and stands next to her, leans on the worktop and gives her a searching look.

'What did you hear?'

Lisa mechanically puts two cups under the espresso machine's spouts. 'Like I said, not much. A few snippets.'

Kreuger crosses his arms. 'They showed a photo of my family. There they were, right in my face, all three of them.'

The coffee beans have run out. Happy with this excuse to delay her reaction, Lisa adds some more. Then she gathers her courage.

'Do you have three children?'

'Two,' he says. 'A boy and a girl. Around the same age as your daughter.'

'Nice, a boy and a girl. We call that a king's wish, don't we?' He must have noticed the fake enthusiasm in her voice.

'That's what they say, yes.' It doesn't sound like a wish that came true.

There's a silence, which Lisa breaks by pressing a button. The coffee beans are milled with an enormous clatter. When they're ready, she presses another button and the coffee streams into the two cups. What does Kreuger want from her? He is

SIMONE VAN DER VLUGT

restless; perhaps he's looking for distractions. The problem is that having a conversation with him is like taking a walk through a minefield. She can't ask him anything about his wife, but perhaps she can talk about his children. They've probably been placed with a foster family or are in a children's home.

'Do you miss them?' she asks, feeling like she's jumping off a mountain blindfolded.

The crushing grip on her arm comes as no surprise.

'And why wouldn't I miss them? Eh? Why do you think I wouldn't miss my own children? Because I've got a criminal record? Maybe you can't imagine it, but I do have feelings. Did you think I didn't have any feelings, you filthy bitch?'

His shouting fills the kitchen. Lisa is scared, but she doesn't shrink back, look down or begin to sob.

With all the self-control she can muster, she sticks out her bandaged hand and lays it on his arm.

'Of course you have feelings,' she says gently. 'And of course you miss your children.'

His rage disappears just as quickly as it surfaced. His face contorts, and the vacant expression returns to his eyes.

'I'm not allowed to see them any more,' he says tonelessly. 'Never again. Can you imagine that?

Their own father? But that didn't matter to the judge. I'm forbidden from seeing them.'

'How terrible for you . . .'

'Yes.' A confused expression appears on his face, as though he doesn't understand quite what he's doing here.

'My ex tried to take Anouk away from me,' Lisa says.

Kreuger massages his forehead with his thumb.

'I told you that he was jealous, didn't I?' She offers Kreuger one of the cups of coffee. He takes it but doesn't drink. 'That jealousy of his ruined our lives. He was jealous of everything, particularly that I had a career and he didn't. He was a manager at a large supermarket, but got made redundant when they restructured. Suddenly he was at home and had all the time in the world to get involved in what I was doing. I was working at a research lab in Utrecht and carpooling with a colleague. A nice guy, but just a colleague. I never thought that Mark would make a fuss about it. At first he didn't, but after he lost his job he started to worry about everything. I reassured him that he could trust me. But he didn't. It only got better when I became pregnant with Anouk.'

Lisa sips from her coffee. Their eyes make contact for a moment and then she looks down.

In a quiet, toneless voice, she tells him about the

post-natal depression that overcame her after Anouk was born, about the dark, dead-end world she inhabited at that time.

'Mark looked after me really well. Even though he'd found a job by then, he took over all my chores: doing the shopping, taking Anouk for her check-ups, you name it. In the meantime, my world became smaller and smaller. My whole life took place inside the house. In hindsight I realise that was what Mark wanted. Finally he had me all to himself.'

She recounts her difficult struggle to escape from her isolation. Mark persuaded her not to go to a psychiatrist, which he thought was just an expensive way of grousing. Mark couldn't understand why she would want to share her thoughts and feelings with a stranger, when her husband was there for her the whole time. He found it insulting, wounding, completely unnecessary. And, what's more, they couldn't afford it.

This was how Mark became the only thing she could cling to as she sank further and further into a deep sea of depression. The tide turned when she joined some internet forums. She ordered anti-depressants from an online chemist and slowly rediscovered the world around her again – only to find that Mark was leading a double life.

'He was cheating on you,' Kreuger states.

'Not only that: he had two sons with that woman.' Lisa's voice sounds dull. 'When I announced that I wanted a divorce, he became furious and threatened to take Anouk away from me. It wouldn't have been that difficult for him, because he'd printed all my correspondence from those forums and saved the invoices for the anti-depressants. I was terrified he'd get sole custody of Anouk.'

'But he didn't. Of course he didn't – they always let the mothers keep the children.' There is an aggressive undertone to Kreuger's voice.

'Not always.' Lisa lifts the espresso cup to her mouth and takes a sip. 'And Mark didn't take it to court. He left Anouk with me. Actually, he dumped both of us.'

13

Senta's greatest dream had always been to become a journalist. Preferably for a big, respected newspaper. But once she was employed by one, she realised that the magazine world was much more attractive to her. She didn't hesitate to make the change and never regretted it. One promotion followed another, with Senta making editor-in-chief of one of the biggest women's magazines before her fortieth birthday.

Getting a good interview requires special skill. Anyone can fire off a series of questions, but you need to be able to do more than this to have a good conversation. Many journalists make the mistake of talking too much themselves, when all they really need to bring to the room is empathy. The only way to think up good leading questions is through trying to understand the interviewee

– and the self-knowledge prompted by such questions will lead the interviewee, in turn, to give answers that make for remarkable reading.

This was what had happened with Alexander Riskens. A writer who led a fairly reclusive life, he wasn't known for his generosity in giving interviews, and it had taken a lot of effort to get him to agree to talk to someone. He had consented only on the condition that she, the editor-in-chief, should do the interview, and she was happy to oblige: she had been a fan of his work for years and wouldn't have dreamed of passing it on to one of her colleagues.

It had been an exciting afternoon. Alexander turned out to be a friendly man who didn't like to talk about himself, making for a tough start. It took three quarters of an hour before she began to win his confidence and could progress from clichéd questions to deeper emotional matters.

She had managed by avoiding the taboo topics, such as the deaths of his wife and young daughter, and questioning him only the subjects that he raised himself. At the beginning this meant that they just talked about his work, and about the writer's block that had paralysed him.

At a certain point they almost imperceptibly slipped into the subject of his private life, and finally there was such a good rapport between them that

Senta found it difficult to bring the interview to a close. Alexander seemed to feel the same way, because he invited her to have lunch with him in a cosy restaurant in the village. She had accepted the invitation, even though alarm bells had begun to ring in her head, and all her senses were telling her she'd have been better off driving back to Amstelveen as quickly as possible.

But she didn't. They went to the restaurant and talked for hours, off the record of course.

Senta knew she had entered a danger zone. She was falling in love with this man; perhaps she was already in love with him, with every minute spent in his company just fuelling these feelings.

In the restaurant she had kept her left hand in sight at all times, so that the white gold wedding ring with its small diamond couldn't escape his notice: a last attempt to keep something of a barrier in place. If you'd asked her a year later what the conversation had been about, what they'd eaten and drunk that afternoon, she wouldn't have had a clue.

She sat there looking at him as if she were bewitched. And vice versa. That first smile of recognition, that first special glance – she saved everything in her memory, larger than life. Not that they were flirting with each other. There was no question of double entendres or teasing – just a calm conversation, with a natural accord that rendered such nonsense unnecessary.

After a while they both fell silent and listened to a song playing in the background.

He looked right inside her. *I want you*, his gaze said. *I love you.*

That's a bit quick, don't you think? her eyes answered.

I don't need any more time.

Senta dropped her eyes, as shy as a teenager, but not before she had conveyed an answer. He pushed a beer mat towards her and she wrote down her number.

I've been punished, Senta thinks; this coma is my punishment. Nothing happens without a reason. Please, God, can we make a pact? If you let me wake up, I promise I'll do the right thing, I really promise. Just let me wake up . . .

14

Police are still hunting escaped psychiatric prisoner Mick Kreuger, who disappeared on Sunday afternoon during an escorted day-release. Despite television appeals for help in tracing the man, and the allocation of extra manpower, nothing is known of his whereabouts. Kreuger was responsible for the death of his 25-year-old escort at a petrol station on Sunday afternoon; surveillance cameras recorded the convicted criminal's violent assault. In the last few hours, the body of a 52-year-old woman has been found in her home, and the police have issued a statement saying that the circumstances are suspicious. RTL has learned that a man fitting Kreuger's description was sighted in the area shortly before the discovery of the body.

After the *RTL News* there's the eight o'clock news, *The Heart of Holland* and various talk shows, all of which lead with Kreuger's escape.

Lisa and Anouk follow the coverage, but Kreuger doesn't seem bothered by this. Without appearing to pay them even a minute amount of attention, he sits on the edge of the sofa, though Lisa knows he is watching their every move.

Anouk, exhausted from coughing, leans against her. 'I want to go to bed, Mummy,' she mumbles, her eyes already closed.

After a brief hesitation, Lisa asks Kreuger if he minds her putting her daughter to bed.

Kreuger slowly turns his head towards her. He seems vacant, as though he has been in a completely different world and is slowly re-entering reality.

After rubbing his face with his hands a few times, he mutters that that's fine.

Lisa is overcome with an immense feeling of relief. She'll let Anouk sleep in her bed and shut the door firmly behind them. Behind the closed door, they'll be able to escape from the atmosphere of constant threat. Kreuger will probably sleep on the sofa, watchful of everything happening outside the house, the television on all night.

She starts to get up, but Kreuger's voice stops her. 'You'll both sleep in the basement tonight.'

Lisa cannot hide her astonishment. 'In the basement?'

Kreuger turns back to the television programme without any further comment.

'But . . . the basement is much too damp for Anouk. And the light's broken – you can't see your hand in front of your face at night.'

'You can put down a mattress and bedding,' is Kreuger's only response.

Lisa pauses, panicked. There's not a lot she can do. Leaving Anouk alone down there in the dark is obviously out of the question, so she'll have to go with her, even though it's still early in the evening.

'She can sleep on the sofa for a while first,' she mutters.

'Whatever,' Kreuger says absently.

'Do I have to go into the basement? No, Mummy. I don't really have to go to the basement, do I?' Anouk looks at her mother with anxious eyes.

There's no point in upsetting her. With a bit of luck, she'll fall asleep on the sofa.

'No, of course not – you're going to sleep on the sofa. We'll put the cushion down like this and then you'll get under your blanket. Isn't that a cosy nest?'

Anouk turns on to her side cautiously. 'You mustn't go away.'

'I'm not going away. I'll stay with you the whole night.'

Anouk's eyes glide over to Kreuger, and she gives her mother a questioning look.

'He's staying here for a while.' To Lisa's own surprise her voice sounds steady and neutral.

'Doesn't he have a home?' Anouk yawns, her mouth unashamedly wide open.

Lisa hurriedly bends down and kisses her cheek.

'Shh, go to sleep. Good girl, eyes closed. Sleep tight, darling.'

'Sing to me . . .'

Barely managing the tune, Lisa begins the song that is part of Anouk's bedtime ritual, but Kreuger puts an abrupt stop to it.

'Can't you shut up? I'm trying to watch this!'

The silence that follows is total. The shock makes Anouk's small body tense up.

Lisa gives her a reassuring smile. She mouths the song until the end, and Anouk soundlessly moves her lips along.

Then they have a kiss and a cuddle.

'I love you,' she whispers into Anouk's ear.

Anouk mouths the same back.

Hours later, Lisa starts from sleep when a hand roughly shakes her shoulder.

'Bedtime,' a voice above her says.

She gets up. The right half of her body has cramp from having slept in the small space left on the sofa by Anouk, who is snoring gently.

'Get a move on!' Pale and irritable, Kreuger pulls her arm, and Lisa, suddenly wide awake, stands up.

'Do we really have to go to the basement?'

'You've got ten minutes to get the mattresses and bedding there. I'll stay with her.'

With an impatient shake of the head, he gestures for Lisa to hurry up.

Still dizzy from standing up so quickly, she goes upstairs on autopilot. The mattress on the double bed in her bedroom is too heavy to carry on her own, and her hand is hurting, so she takes Anouk's mattress instead and pushes it down the stairs. She pulls a second mattress from the spare bedroom and gives it a shove too, so that it slides down the stairs into the hall. Pillows, duvets and pyjamas in her arms, she goes downstairs. Within ten minutes, everything is in the dark, damp basement.

She lugs Anouk down the narrow stairway with difficulty. Kreuger watches her every move. As Lisa is settling them in, his tall shape appears at the top of the basement stairs, and he looks down at her.

'OK, I'll let you out again tomorrow morning.'

Before Lisa can say anything, the door closes, and darkness is all around them. The light fixture is broken – one of the things on the to-do list of household repairs.

The key grates in the lock and she sinks down next to Anouk on the mattress.

Her daughter has woken up but falls asleep again when she hears her mother's voice soothing her. Thank God. There's no way they can escape from the basement. High above them there's a window, but it's too small even to stick your head through. It does let in a little of the dusky light, but, because there's no outside lighting at the back of the house, it doesn't amount to much. She'd be best off going to sleep; she desperately needs rest. Who knows what tomorrow will bring?

The police, she thinks, full of desperate hope. Please let the police turn up.

She feels for her pyjamas with her good hand and gets undressed. She crawls under the duvet and wraps an arm around Anouk.

Above them there's a rush of water, and then she hears a gurgling in the pipe that runs down into the basement. Kreuger is taking a shower.

Lisa rolls on to her back and listens to the sounds upstairs: the flush of the toilet, Kreuger's footsteps resounding on the landing, the protesting squeak of the cupboards as he opens them. Not long afterwards it grows quiet, and she hears the creaking of a bed. Her bed.

15

The basement had been Mark's territory. There was enough space to store plenty of stuff; he'd hung shelves on the walls and filled them with all the rubbish Lisa herself would have thrown away, but which he couldn't bear to part with: old, rusty tools that he never used, broken appliances like vacuum cleaners and radios that he was planning to repair, boxes of corks, bin-bag ties, used batteries – he saved everything. He also used the garage for storing larger things, such as damaged garden chairs, and tiles in various sizes and colours that might one day come in handy.

When they broke up, Lisa put everything out with the rubbish. It was a relief in more ways than one. Once Mark and all his mess had gone, there was light and space in the house, but also a terrible emptiness.

She knows exactly what's in the basement – there's nothing here that she can use. The once-packed space is as good as empty, making it a perfect prison cell. Before her clearing-up spree, she and Anouk would never have been able to fit the mattresses into the cellar. But, in that case, Kreuger might have taken more drastic measures to get them out of his way.

She forces herself to think about something else. About Mark. Even though they're separated, he still calls regularly, making all kinds of suggestions as an excuse to contact them. She doesn't entirely mind; she needs to hear his voice too. But unfortunately he also turns up unexpectedly. She can't cope with seeing him, not yet. She hasn't let go of him enough to be comfortable with that.

There's a strong chance that he'll turn up on the doorstep tomorrow. Sweat breaks out on her forehead at the thought: how on earth are they going to stop him from coming in? Mark isn't someone who'll accept no for an answer. Luckily she didn't get the chance to tell him that Anouk was ill; otherwise he'd certainly have come. Whatever else she thinks of him, he's undeniably a good father and he loves his daughter to bits.

'Mark . . .' Lisa mumbles into the darkness.

Deep in the night, Anouk wakes suddenly in the middle of a bad dream. When she sees how dark it is around them, she begins to scream. Lisa shoots upright, feels for her daughter, gathers her in and comforts her.

'Quiet now, quiet now, Mummy's here. Don't scream, Anouk, everything's fine.'

Relieved that she's not alone, Anouk presses into her. 'Light,' she says in a trembling voice.

'The light's broken, darling. But there's no need to be frightened, I'm here with you.'

'Light!' There's panic in Anouk's voice, but Lisa manages to quieten her.

'Let's cuddle up together. The dark isn't scary, it really isn't.'

'Where are we?'

Lisa feels Anouk tense up next to her.

'In the basement,' she says simply. 'You know, Daddy's room.'

'With all that mess.'

'Yes, but the mess has gone now. I tidied it all up, remember?'

'I want to phone Daddy,' Anouk says with her thumb in her mouth. 'Daddy needs to fix the light. I want to go to my own bed.'

Lisa sighs gently. 'Me too, but we can't, darling.'

There's a short silence, then the sound of Anouk's voice again in the darkness. 'Is that scary man still there?'

He's in my bed, Lisa thinks bitterly, but replies

in a cheerier tone, 'Yes, but it won't last much longer.'

Another silence, then Anouk asks, 'Is he a child molester, Mummy?'

Despite everything, Lisa has to laugh. 'No, he's not a child molester. But you're right, he is a strange man. That's why we have to do exactly what he says; otherwise he'll get angry.'

'And then he starts hitting really hard, doesn't he?' There's a concerned tone in Anouk's voice, and Lisa feels her daughter's small hand glide over her face. She kisses it and says nothing, afraid her voice will betray her emotions.

With gentle force, she manages to get Anouk to lie down again; then she pulls the duvet over her shoulders with a nurturing gesture. She curls up against her daughter and sings softly to her until she dozes off. Lisa lies there, sleepless, until the first morning light enters through the tiny window.

She gets up and makes a thorough inspection of the basement. Just as she'd expected, there's nothing that she can use as a weapon or to raise the alarm in any way. There's just an old radio of Mark's.

Lisa plugs it in and turns a dial, and to her surprise she hears a noise. Amazingly, it works.

She searches feverishly for a news programme but gets only adverts. Although she has to wait at least fifteen minutes before the six o'clock news begins, there's something about Kreuger almost as soon as the programme begins.

> *A special team from the national police force is working around the clock to track down escaped convict Mick Kreuger. This special unit has been set up in view of the danger the man poses to the community. Yesterday, Kreuger killed two people during his escape, and today it has been made public that he was responsible for the violent murders not only of his ex-wife and her partner, but also of his children.*

Her ear pressed to the radio, Lisa sits down on a stool. She doesn't dare turn up the volume for fear of waking Anouk or of Kreuger hearing it, but she doesn't want to miss a word. The newsreader continues without intonation, his voice as neutral as if he were reading a traffic report. The stool seems smaller and smaller, until Lisa almost falls from it and needs to support herself by placing her good hand on the shelving unit.

My God. He really did murder his wife. And not just her but also his own children. Violently. What does that mean?

An image of two large hands closing around a child's throat appears before her eyes. Who would do something like that? What can go so wrong in your head that you become capable of squeezing the life out of a helpless child?

Behind her, Anouk mutters in her sleep, and Lisa closes her eyes so as not to be swept away in a wave of despair and helplessness.

16

A large part of the morning has passed before the key grinds in the lock and the basement door swings open. Lisa and Anouk are sitting side by side, leaning against the wall, the duvets pulled up around them.

Kreuger looks down on them like a medieval lord and nods at the stairs.

Lisa stands up stiffly and helps Anouk to her feet. The child is quiet and pale, but not coughing any more. Thank God the antibiotics have started to take effect.

Maybe Kreuger will leave today, Lisa thinks hopefully. Surely he can't stay here for ever. She could offer him money and clothing to speed him on his way. If necessary she could take him over the border in her car. Whatever he wants.

New-found hope takes over, and, in a better

frame of mind, she helps Anouk up the stairs. The television is on in the sitting room, but the curtains are still drawn. Behind the thin fabric, the sun is attempting to shine, but this only serves to highlight the chaos inside. Pages of newspaper have been tossed all around the sitting room – on the sofa, on the floor, on the coffee table – as though he had literally been spreading the news.

The kitchen is a disaster: the worktop is covered in empty packets and the floor littered with crumbs, cheese rinds and bits of eggshell. Pretty much the entire contents of the fridge have been spread out over the worktop, and there's a strong smell of coffee and fried eggs. His lordship obviously feels at home. Suddenly Lisa is less convinced that he'll leave any time soon, and the disappointment translates itself into a throbbing pain behind her eyes.

As Kreuger whistles his way through the sitting room, Lisa goes over to the worktop, prepares breakfast for Anouk and herself and takes the meal to the small wooden table in the kitchen, rather than to the dining table in the other room.

'I'm not that hungry, Mummy,' Anouk says quietly.

'Me neither.' Lisa chews reluctantly on a cheese sandwich. The bread forms a sticky ball in her mouth, which she has to wash down with a few large gulps of tea. 'Try to eat what you can. A few mouthfuls is enough. Can you manage some milk?'

By way of an answer, Anouk picks up her glass with both hands and drinks it all. She gives her mother a triumphant look. Lisa smiles approvingly.

Anouk leans in towards her conspiratorially and asks, 'Do we have to stay here today?'

Over my dead body, Lisa thinks. This is still my house.

'No,' she says. 'I'm going to have a word with that man. Maybe we can take him somewhere.'

'Where?'

To prison, Lisa thinks. Or a very deep pit.

She shrugs. 'Somewhere where they can't find him.'

'He's hiding here,' Anouk surmises. 'From the police.'

Lisa cannot deny it.

'Can't the police find him, Mummy?'

'No. They don't seem to be able to.'

Anouk looks out of the kitchen window and Lisa gives her a worried glance. What is going through her head, and how great is the chance she'll be damaged by it? Anouk has had to watch her mother being hit until she bled and threatened with a knife; and she's had to spend the night locked up in a dark basement. Although all the ingredients for long-term problems are there, if Kreuger leaves today hopefully the harm shouldn't be too great.

Anouk might be frightened of strangers for a while, but in time she should be able to forget the incident.

And it could all have been much worse. How can she protect her child from everything that she fears?

By not holding back cautiously any longer, she realises. She has to take matters into her own hands and convince Kreuger that he'd be better off leaving.

'Mum?' Lisa is jolted from her thoughts by Anouk's hopeful voice.

'Yes?'

'Can you please bring my Barbies downstairs?'

It's a perfect domestic scene: Anouk in the sitting room playing with her Barbie dolls, Kreuger sunk into his newspaper and Lisa cleaning up the kitchen. Once she's finished, she automatically switches on the espresso machine, and the smell of ground beans fills the kitchen.

'Yes, coffee!' Kreuger shouts from the sitting room.

Lisa stands in the door opening. 'Milk or sugar?'

Kreuger shakes his head without looking up.

Or would you like something else in it? Lisa adds in her thoughts. Rat poison, an overdose of sleeping pills, a mixture of all the dregs from the bottles of strong medicine . . .

As a lab technician, she knows plenty about

poisons. She works for a research institute that offers analytical support to companies developing cosmetics and medicines. It's her job to analyse the base materials and end-products before they're released.

You don't need to be a Russian spy to be poisoned to death. Medicines and cosmetics are full of poison. The slogan 'dermatologically tested' on packaging is usually meaningless. The words suggest that it's a safe and skin-friendly product that has been carefully tested, while the research often isn't any more thorough than an employee rubbing the cream into their skin and waiting to see whether they get a rash. The term 'dermatologically tested' isn't legally defined; anybody can put it on their product. A pot of cream that costs the earth and contains innocent-sounding 'cleansing plant extracts' doesn't have to say on the label that the red algae used are poisonous.

What Lisa does is conduct thorough research, provide information to consumers through publications and attempt to bring some transparency to the chemical jargon of cosmetics manufacturers.

At present, she's conducting a crusade against companies that include Botox in their products, emptying their customers' purses without the ingredient having any effect on wrinkles. If a cream can actually change your skin structure, it's a medicine, and medicines can be obtained only on prescription.

Lisa stares into mid-air. Poison is everywhere, in everything that you use or take. Around ninety per cent of poisonings occur in the home: a burger that's a little too raw or a chicken fillet that's been out of the fridge all day could be enough. The problem with food, though, is that it's hard to ensure the poison goes to the right person. The odds are that Kreuger would give that piece of chicken to her. Or, worse still, to Anouk.

No, she won't take that risk. She has to approach this more intelligently. Would he notice if she put something in his coffee? Rat poison is naturally very effective, but she doesn't have any. She does have an ant trap, but how much ant poison would you need to topple a grown man? And what if he susses what she's trying to do and spits out his coffee right away?

With a sigh, she takes two coffee cups from the machine and carries them into the sitting room. There's still time for desperate measures, but she decides to try talking first.

As she sets down the coffee on the table in front of Kreuger, she attempts to catch a glimpse of what he's reading. Today's paper has been delivered.

'Is there any news?' she asks casually.

'No, not really.'

'No new developments, then,' Lisa establishes.

The chuckle as he looks up is horrible. 'They have no idea where I am, if that's what you mean. So actually there is news. Very good news, even.'

'You know yourself that the police will be careful about the information they give out, so as not to sabotage their efforts.'

Her comment doesn't have much effect on him. With an airy gesture, Kreuger shuts the newspaper. 'But if they knew where I was, we'd have noticed.'

Lisa can't say much to this.

'You don't know,' she says finally. 'They might be closer than you think.'

'They've already been close. Yesterday afternoon, they drove up and down the embankment.'

'The police?' An amazed expression appears on Anouk's face.

'The police. Of course they had no idea they were so warm. They weren't looking for me.'

There's a pause.

'Who for, then?' Lisa dares to ask.

Kreuger opens the paper and looks for the page with the regional news. 'It says someone drove their car into the canal yesterday afternoon. Not that far from here.'

He obligingly turns the paper towards Lisa. Her eyes fly over the short article containing an account of the incident. As she reads the piece, her breathing gets faster and faster.

According to the report, yesterday afternoon a 43-year-old woman drove her car off the embankment and into the canal. She lost control of the vehicle when speeding around a bend near the village of Appeltern. The car ended up in the water, and by the time the eyewitness, a man walking his dog, arrived on the scene the vehicle had sunk. The man dived into the water, brought the woman to the surface and resuscitated her until the ambulance arrived. The woman was taken to hospital, unconscious. According to the latest reports, she was still in a coma.

17

Senta is torn from her slumber by a jingle. Someone has put a radio next to her bed. A happy voice reaches her ears, then the latest hits, interspersed with jokes and bursts of laughter from the programme's presenter.

It's too fast for Senta, it's too much, it's giving her a headache. Can't someone turn off that horrible noise?

But suddenly the chatter and the raucous laughter stop, and she feels herself gently being picked up and rocked by reassuring sounds. She knows this song: she's got the CD.

She sings along quietly in her under-water world. Not a moment's hesitation. And from somewhere within her memory's deep vaults a name pops up. Not the name of the singer, but of someone she associates with this song. A forbidden name, one that could damage her pact with God.

In her panic she flees towards other thoughts, memories from the time when her children were small, and then back to the present. The last holiday they took together in Italy, when Niels had felt he was too old to go with them and they'd tried desperately to convince him otherwise. For three long weeks he'd sat in a chair with his iPod on, looking bored. He'd scuppered all their plans for daytrips and moved only when there was food on the table. Denise had enjoyed the holiday. Whereas at home it was difficult to get her to do anything, whether it was a board game or going into town with Senta, on holiday, without the constant presence of her girlfriends, she'd been eager to spend time with her mother.

Senta had enjoyed having her daughter to herself again. At home Senta led her own life: there was a TV in every room, and often they'd all be watching different things. For years the summer holiday had been the only time they really got together as a family.

That Niels hadn't wanted to come had been a rude wake-up call for Senta. Her children had grown up: Niels was already seventeen; Denise fourteen; and Jelmer, the youngest, eleven and going to secondary school next year. Soon she'd find herself alone in Italy with Frank.

She had stood in front of the mirror and taken a good look at herself – this time without first closing the bathroom blinds, so that the harsh light was not subdued. She wasn't happy with what she saw. But she'd still had a big party for her fortieth, and adopted the nonchalant attitude of someone unconcerned about having left her thirties behind for good. Forty was the new thirty, and that was how she planned to behave.

In her heart she had known that forty wasn't a new beginning and that from now on things could only go downhill. Slowly, yes, but inevitably too.

Just after her forty-third birthday she began to dream about the past. Each night she returned to her university years, to the easy-going, unattached girl she had once been. And when she woke up, it took her some time to realise that she was now twice the age she had been then.

Suddenly time seemed to go more quickly, and she no longer took pleasure in looking through old photo albums or watching videos of her children when they were small; the tenderness that she usually felt now went hand in hand with a suffocating feeling of nostalgia.

She was middle-aged. In a few years she'd no

longer be able to compete with radiant thirty-year-olds, and she'd no longer be able to attract admiring glances from passing men.

She hadn't expected to feel so depressed by it. Perhaps this was why she had been so susceptible to Alexander's charms. Despite his boldness, Alexander hadn't moved too fast. He'd taken the time to get to know her, and after a few weeks, when they'd gone to bed together for the first time, his caresses had been tender and careful. He knew exactly where and how much.

After twenty-one years of marriage this was something Frank still hadn't managed. And once she started to compare her husband with her lover, she found it impossible to stop. She knew very well that in the first stages of falling in love, a lover's qualities shine brightly, and that the husband you've spent half your life with dulls in comparison, like an overexposed photograph. She'd commissioned too many magazine articles on the subject, read too many pieces, heard too many stories, not to recognise the truth of the clichés.

No, after twenty-one years, Frank wasn't as attentive as he had been in the beginning. Alexander, on the other hand, held open every door for her, pulled out her chair if she wanted to sit down, didn't just slice and scoff the garlic bread as Frank did but offered it to her first.

While these things had never really bothered her before, now she wondered on an almost daily basis who had come up with the idea that people should be monogamous. Monogamy wasn't a biological imperative needed to keep the species alive; even in the animal world it was quite rare. It was a rule someone had come up with that every mortal was sorely tempted to break.

It wasn't that she didn't love Frank any more. The advantage of so many years of marriage was that the rush of passionate love had been replaced by a close companionship and intimacy – qualities that the young colleagues in her team considered middle-aged and boring, but that had a value Senta certainly didn't underestimate.

The problem was that every five years or so you change, like a snake shedding its skin. For years she and Frank had shed their skins at the same time, got to know each other again and held each other's interest. But recently Senta had felt stuck in her old skin, however hard she tried to wriggle out of it. And Frank looked on without lifting a finger to help her, without even realising that she was slowly suffocating.

18

The black print dances before Lisa's eyes. It is as though she can sense a deep abyss, and instinctively she grabs the edge of the table.

'Appeltern, that's this place, isn't it?' Kreuger asks with interest.

Lisa only nods.

'Just fancy that. If I'd gone out on to the street yesterday afternoon, I'd have walked right into the police's arms. It is much too risky to leave the house. I'd be better off waiting here for a while, don't you think?' Kreuger says breezily.

'Yes,' Lisa admits. 'I think you're right.'

He looks at her in amazement.

'At least for the time being,' she continues. 'I won't try to make it difficult.'

He studies her carefully. 'Very good.'

'But I can imagine you have a plan. I mean, you

can't stay here for ever. Do you have any idea where you want to go? I could drive you; it's not a problem. I have a car, as you know. Or you could borrow it if you—'

Kreuger's laugh stops her mid-sentence.

'Maybe,' he says. 'I'm not sure yet, but perhaps I'll take you up on your offer. Money, a car, yeah, that would certainly help. Maybe I'll take you with me. Or just your little girl. Now that I think about it, that seems like a good idea . . .'

His eyes grow thoughtful as Lisa's become wild.

'No!' she says furiously. 'You stay away from my daughter, do you hear? I—'

All the friendliness vanishes from his face.

'I'll do what I want,' he says quietly. 'And you'll cooperate, get it? You won't make things difficult. You're not about to kick off, are you?'

His gaze descends to Anouk, who is busy laying her bikinied Barbies on sun loungers.

'No, of course not. I'm sorry I lost control.' The hoarse, hunted tone of her voice sounds like a total stranger's – someone she would rather not know. Meek-as-a-lamb Lisa, who lets herself be toyed with, seems like someone else. When Kreuger gets up and turns to her, she expects to see the scorn and contempt she feels for herself reflected in his face. She's not prepared for his pity and the gentle voice he uses.

'I do understand. Don't think I don't understand, Lisa.'

Hearing him say her name sends shivers down her spine. The way he says it gives her hope, even though she knows she mustn't trust him.

'You won't harm her, will you?' she whispers. 'She's all I have.'

Behind her Anouk brings Ken on to the scene. 'Who's coming for a swim?' a deep voice asks, and the Barbies get up to dive into the sea with Ken.

'She's ill,' Lisa says quietly. 'She needs a doctor.'

'She doesn't seem that ill to me.'

'Appearances can be deceptive – listen to her breathing.'

As though sensing the importance of the moment, Anouk coughs loudly a few times.

'She's got penicillin,' Kreuger says.

'But if that isn't enough, she has to—'

'We'll see how it goes,' Kreuger interrupts. 'At the moment she's fine. Look how nicely she's playing.' The tenderness on his face turns into something tired and infinitely sad.

What is he thinking about? What images are flashing before his eyes?

'My daughter had some of those pink horses,' he says. 'She would comb them all the time. What do you call them again?'

'My Little Pony?' Lisa asks cautiously.

'Yes, that was it. Little Ponies.'

Quick, say something else to keep the conversation going. 'I think all the girls like those. Anouk has a few.'

Kreuger sits there staring into a world that Lisa cannot see but that she can imagine. What should she say? Maybe she'd better hold her tongue.

But Kreuger doesn't give her the chance. 'You know what happened, don't you? What I did?' He looks at her, and his glare forces her to answer.

'Yes.'

'How?'

'You mean, how I do know?'

He nods impatiently.

Her confession comes out as a whisper. 'There's a radio downstairs.'

'Then you know exactly what kind of monster I am, what I'm capable of.' There is a bitterness behind his words. Yet it doesn't seem to be aimed at Lisa, so she cautiously continues.

'I believe we can all find ourselves in situations in which we lose the run of ourselves. When we do things we wouldn't normally do. Sometimes circumstances drive us to it,' Lisa carefully offers.

'Or people.'

'Yes, or people.'

Unexpectedly he pushes back his chair and stands up so that they are facing one another. Lisa represses the temptation to step back and increase the distance between them. Her heart begins to beat more quickly.

Kreuger's face comes very close. 'Have you ever been in a situation like that?'

'I tried to murder my ex,' Lisa mumbles, barely comprehensible.

She has his attention. He tilts his head slightly and stares at her. 'What did you do?'

Lisa avoids his eyes, but it is as though Kreuger sucks her gaze towards him. His eyes tear the words from her mouth. Now that she's said this, she'll have to speak – she won't get away with this vague confession.

'I ran him over.'

Kreuger whistles softly. 'Did he die?'

'No – he was seriously injured and went to hospital, but he survived.'

There's something of respect in his expression. 'And you got away with it?'

Lisa runs her hand through her hair nervously. 'Yes. I drove off really fast. There weren't any witnesses. Mark never found out that I was the one who ran him over, though he suspected it. He used to give me a funny look whenever we talked about his accident . . .'

'And then?'

'Then we broke up,' Lisa says simply. 'He

understood he'd overstepped the mark and that I'd kill him the next time.'

'Really? You would have done it again?'

'Definitely.' The wound on her hand throbs; her lip has opened again and stings. 'I can understand and forgive just like the next person, but there are limits.'

19

Lisa pulls on her jeans and a clean white top. She hurries because she hates leaving Anouk with Kreuger, even for such a short time. She gives her hair a perfunctory comb with her fingers and runs downstairs. As her foot reaches the bottom step, she hears the sound of a car in the distance.

Her hand grips the banister tightly and, holding her breath, she peers through the frosted glass of the front door to try to see something. Is it Mark, or her mother?

Please let it be one of them, she pleads inwardly. No, for God's sake let it not be one of them!

Torn between hope and fear, she waits until Kreuger notices the sound, but the hall door is closed. Lisa tiptoes to the front door. Something orange shines through the glass. It's the post van. Can she do anything? Thoughts race through her brain. As long as the door is locked, she can't do anything. Shouting a warning to the elderly, rather deaf postman through the letter box is much too risky. All the conversations she's ever had with him have been shouted comments about the weather.

The post van stops in front of her house, and Lisa looks around, at her wit's end. Pen, paper! She has to write a note, hurry!

Too late: the crunch of footsteps on the gravel announces the postman's approach. His shape pops up in front of the door, like a guardian angel from another world – out of reach. 'Postman! Postman!' she calls through the letter box as loudly as she can. She sees him rummaging around in his bag and puts her hand through the letter box in an attempt to attract his attention. The next moment she can hear him laughing and feels the post being pressed into her hand.

The sound of footsteps retreating is a drum roll announcing the end of the world – her world.

She goes into the sitting room in despair. Anouk is kneading Play-Doh at the dining table, and Kreuger is following her work closely. He pays the same intense attention to the letter in Lisa's hand.

'Post,' he says, in a tone that betrays he hadn't thought of this possibility.

The kitchen is suffused with the smell of toasted sandwiches and fresh coffee. It is just after one thirty in the afternoon. The morning slipped by in relative peace and quiet, and Lisa notices that she feels less tense. The radio is on, the curtains are still closed, and it's stuffy and warm inside, but she's less fearful of being murdered. Nothing is certain in the company of a psychopath, but at this moment it is hard to imagine that the man sitting opposite her murdered his family. It's best just not to think about it. Every time her thoughts take the wrong turn, she redirects them to the next morning. The postman will be back then.

Anouk decides she wants to finger-paint, and soon she's absorbed in this.

'Emily loved that stuff too.' Kreuger takes a bite of his sandwich. 'After five minutes she'd be totally covered in paint. And the table, the chair and the floor.'

Lisa smiles in recognition at the image, until she remembers that she's smiling at the image of a small, dead girl.

As though he can read her thoughts, Kreuger suddenly begins to share. 'Jeffrey was two and Emily was four when my wife left me. I'd already known for a while that Angelique was seeing someone else – I just knew.' His voice takes on the defensive tone of someone who assumes that everything they say will be treated with scepticism. 'A man can sense when he's being cheated on. I asked her about it, but she refused to talk to me. She just disappeared off upstairs without saying a thing. When she turned her back on me, something snapped inside. I felt so unbelievably humiliated by having to run around after her, and yes, then I lost control of myself. I threw her down the stairs. In front of the children – that wasn't so clever. But I couldn't think clearly: it was as though I was only fragments of myself, as though you'd only have to pull a single thread for me to fall apart. And she kept pulling at that thread.' He pauses for a while and then continues. 'Angelique had a few bruises and concussion. She got up, took the children to her parents' and came back the next day with her brother and sister to pick up her stuff. I tried to talk to her, to say sorry, but there was no point. She disappeared from my life without giving me the chance to make it up to her.' Kreuger's voice quavers at the unfairness of the memory. 'The worst thing was that I hardly got to see my children after that. The visiting arrangements were ridiculous: a few hours a fortnight, under strict supervision. The first hour my children stood there staring at me like I was a total stranger who might attack them at any second, and just when they'd finally relaxed the bitch who came to supervise took them away again.' His voice is shaking, and his eyes take on a strange lustre.

Lisa keeps a careful watch on him. 'And then what happened?'

'My life fell to pieces. I'd never cried as much as I did then. My wife was gone, my children were gone, and, as if that wasn't enough, I lost my job too. I sat around at home all day with nothing but problems on my mind. And one day I saw her. She was walking through the town centre with another guy. So I was right. She had been cheating on me with someone else, and now they were walking down the street together. With the children. She was holding Emily's hand, and my little boy was skipping along holding that bastard's hand. All my fuses blew, but I knew I couldn't do much in the middle of the high street. I found out where he lived and drove to that bastard's house. It wasn't that difficult to break in, and then I lay in wait.'

He stops and looks at Lisa to check that she's still listening. She is. One hundred per cent.

'What did you do next?' she asks quietly.

'I murdered them,' he says simply. 'First that prick. He went to the garage. I slipped in behind him and bashed his brains out. Piece of piss – he never knew what hit him. That was a shame, but I couldn't take the risk of it turning into a fight. Angelique would have been warned then.'

'And then you went back into the house.'

Kreuger nods in agreement. 'I'd seen Angelique going upstairs. I got a big knife from the kitchen and went up after her. The children were in the living room, but I could get into the hall through the garage and the utility room without being seen.' An almost dreamy look appears in his eyes. 'I'd murdered her so many times in my fantasies. Each time, I did it slowly, so that she would be aware of what she'd done to me, so that she'd realise it was her own fault she was suffering. But, when it came down to it, it wasn't possible. The children were in the house, and I had to be quick.'

He says it with resolve, as though he'd been dealing with an irritating household chore that he couldn't get out of.

'She saw me coming at her with a knife and began to scream, but downstairs they couldn't hear her over the television. And her screaming soon stopped.' There is satisfaction in Kreuger's voice.

Lisa tries to hide the shivers running down her spine. 'And the children?' she whispers.

Kreuger's expression darkens. He looks up at her with a face that still betrays despair after all this time. 'What else could I do? I knew I wouldn't get away with it and that I'd go to prison for years. What would have happened to Emily and Jeffrey? Think about it: what kind of life would they have had? Their mother murdered, their father in prison, and the two of them sent from foster home to foster home. I did them a service by saving them from that. I did it as fast as I could. I just drew the knife and it was over. I was thinking only about what was best for them. I tried to explain that to the judge too, that I'd been acting in my children's best interests, but he didn't listen.'

Again there is anger in his voice, but it is short-lived. A moment later his eyes are dull, and his voice is tired and depressed.

'Admit it, I couldn't do anything else, could I?' he mutters to himself.

Lisa can only stare at him. That the man sitting opposite her murdered his ex-wife and her boyfriend is terrible, but that he managed to cut his own children's throats is unthinkable.

Most people would react to a story like this with rigid horror. But, for Lisa, it is as though she can share his memories telepathically. She hears the screaming, the pleading, she smells the blood . . .

She breaks out in a sweat; her hands begin to shake, and she takes fast, shallow breaths. She notices that Kreuger is keeping an eye on her, so she tries to keep her facial expression as neutral as possible.

'You know what it's like,' he says, as though they are kindred spirits. 'You tried to murder your husband yourself.'

'It wasn't the same . . .'

'Oh, no? What's the difference?'

Lisa remains silent.

Kreuger leans towards her a little. 'You want to spit at me. I'm such a bastard that I make you feel sick. Do you think you're better than me because you don't have any blood on your hands? You're wrong, darling. We're exactly the same.'

No, we're not, Lisa thinks. We're not at all, you disgusting piece of shit. I would never do anything to my daughter. I would rather leave her with Mark and never see her again than lay a single finger on her.

She doesn't say a word until she notices that Kreuger's face is becoming darker and darker. Fear tightens around her throat.

'Maybe you're right,' she says gently. 'Remember I told you that I suffered from post-natal depression after Anouk was born? That was really heavy. I wasn't myself for months.' She picks up the leftover crust of a toasted sandwich from her plate and nervously breaks it into tiny pieces. 'I couldn't cope. The housework, the baby crying all the time, my body completely broken after the difficult birth . . .'

An encouraging nod from Kreuger helps her to carry on.

'I can't imagine it now, but there was a moment

when I was convinced that Anouk couldn't have ended up with a worse mother than me. Why else would she cry all day and all night? I wondered why on earth I'd thought it necessary to bring a child into the world. Into this polluted, stinking, bad world, where she spent all her time kicking and screaming. One afternoon the bawling got so deep into my head that I couldn't think any more. I took all the sleeping pills that were in the medicine cabinet and the next second I was standing over her cot with a pillow. Just as I started to press it on to Anouk's face, Mark arrived home . . .' Lisa's voice dies away. She keeps her eyes fixed on the plate and the crumbs, so as not to catch the look of understanding and recognition in his eyes.

It remains quiet, and after a while there's nothing else to do but look up. Kreuger is leaning back with an impassive expression on his face.

'He put me into a clinic,' Lisa says simply. 'Not a forced admission: I went voluntarily. I knew I'd try again otherwise. I didn't come home until I was cured, and then I learned how to enjoy Anouk.'

'So you didn't tell me the entire story.'

'It's nothing to be proud of.'

Kreuger's eyes fix on her. 'But you can admit it to a disturbed criminal who murdered his own family.'

'Something like that.'

123

Her honest reply disarms him. He gives her a hypnotic stare – it lasts so long that Lisa begins to feel nervous – but then suddenly he grins. 'We have more in common than I thought.'

'I believe that many people have a dark side. And that there are few people who'll admit how close they've come to the edge.'

Kreuger nods. He believes it, Lisa thinks. That idiot really believes I tried to suffocate my child.

The loud ringing of the telephone breaks the silence like a grenade going off. Lisa jumps up, and Kreuger is so quick to get to his feet that his chair falls over backwards.

He grabs the house telephone, which had been clipped to his belt, and looks at the LCD display.

'Mum,' he reads aloud. 'OK, just pick up. And think before you speak: no hints, no cleverness, no secret messages. Just have a chat, get it? Not too long and not too short.' He hands Lisa the telephone, adding, 'Put it on speaker phone if you like. I know it's impolite, but I'd really like to listen in.'

20

The relationship between body and soul is a strange phenomenon. We know that the soul has a strong capacity to heal the body, but how exactly this occurs is still a mystery. It must have something to do with willpower, with the force you exert to get your body under control.

If you believe that your body won't obey you, how likely is it that your state will change? But if people can think themselves out of recovery, shouldn't they also be able to think themselves better?

Senta holds her breath and concentrates so hard on waking up that it gives her a headache. Then she opens her mouth and screams an order at her soul with all the air she has in her lungs. But the water absorbs her scream, leaving her only with silence. The black hole tugs at her, but Senta resists and kicks frantically, like a drowning man on his way to the surface.

And then, all of a sudden, she is up. When she least expects it, she shoots through the tough membrane that has separated her from the world all this time,

She opens her eyes and looks around, breathing hard. A television hanging from a stand shows a ball game. A ray of golden light streams through the window, giving the room a warm glow.

Very carefully, as though she might damage it irreparably, Senta lifts her hand and holds it in the sunlight. A pleasant warmth caresses her skin. Tears appear in her eyes.

At that moment, a woman with a white coat and a stethoscope around her neck comes into the room. She stops in her tracks when she sees Senta.

The next minute the room is full of doctors and nurses. They look at her and talk among themselves. The woman doctor with the stethoscope sits down on the edge of the bed, takes Senta's hand and asks her how she's feeling.

With difficulty, Senta manages something that resembles 'good'. It's not much more than an 'oo' sound, but they seem to understand.

'I'm Lilian Reynders from Diagnostics.' The doctors looks at her with warm, dark eyes. 'You've kept us on tenterhooks for quite some time, Mrs

Van Dijk. It's good news that you've woken up. Very good news!'

'Where—'

'You're in Intensive Care at the Radboud Hospital in Nijmegen. You had a car accident. Can you remember it?'

Senta looks at the doctor vacantly. A car accident?

'You drove your car into the water. Luckily a passer-by saw it and got you out. Do you remember?'

Her only reaction is an astonished shake of the head.

'It might come back to you,' Dr Reynders says in an effort to comfort her.

Frank and the children run through her head, but she has difficulty in making sounds. Dr Reynders must be a mind reader, because she smiles at her reassuringly.

'We'll inform your family right away. In the meantime we'll run a couple of tests and see how you're doing.'

Senta resigns herself to the succession of activities that follows. They check whether she has regained control of her limbs – she has to move everything and say whether it hurts or not – blood is taken, and then a nurse wheels her away for an MRI scan.

When she is returned to her room, Frank and the children are sitting there waiting for her. As soon as her bed is rolled through the door, they spring to their feet.

'Senta, darling!' Frank takes a step forward and then hesitates. He waits until Senta's bed is back in place before sitting on the edge of it.

The children remain standing, pale and nervous, with tense eyes focused on their mother. Cautiously, as though the slightest touch could send her back into a coma, Frank takes Senta's hand in his and brings it to his lips. 'We were so worried, darling. So terribly worried! Thank God you've woken up.'

Senta produces a weak smile. Her husband doesn't look well: he's as white as chalk, and his red-ringed eyes have bags under them.

Frank tenderly bends over her and kisses her gently on the mouth. 'How do you feel?'

'Tired,' Senta whispers.

'You must be. You've gone through a lot.'

'You could say you've had a lovely, long sleep,' Niels laughs, causing his sister to elbow him in the ribs.

'Behave,' she says angrily.

Senta gives her elder son a reassuring smile. How tall the boy is, standing there at the foot of her bed. He towers over her, all arms and legs. His camouflage clothes and cap worn nonchalantly backwards are a good disguise for the emotional tempest he's been through, but they don't fool his mother.

Impulsively she holds out her arms to him. Niels moves forward and puts his arms around his mother as best he can. There's something awkward about it, but it's the first time they've hugged for a long time. Niels has never been very physical, and he has always shrugged off her attempts at affection with something like impatience.

'I'm glad you're back, Mum,' he says a little hoarsely.

Next Denise rushes into her mother's arms. She wraps herself around Senta and kisses her on the cheek. 'You know what the doctor said? She said you might never wake up!' She stands up and rubs her eyes.

'She didn't say that: you read it on the internet,' her father corrects her. 'I told you not to get carried away by what was on those sites.'

'But it could have happened! Mummy was in a coma!' Denise shouts.

Senta turns to Jelmer, standing silently next to his father. 'Hey, sweetheart,' she manages to say softly. 'How are you?'

Without saying a word, Jelmer climbs up on to the bed and snuggles against her. Senta moves over and wraps her arm around her son. She runs her hand through his dark brown hair and kisses the top of his head. The familiar smell of her child sets off memories of their bedtime ritual: one last cuddle, tight arms around her neck and lots of wet kisses.

How could she have forgotten her family? How distant from them must she have been for that to have happened?

'Don't worry,' she says, gradually recovering her voice. She looks at them one by one. 'I've woken up now and everything's going to be all right.'

With the caution of someone who is not quite convinced, Frank strokes a stray lock of hair from her forehead. 'Can you remember how the accident happened? What on earth where you doing on that embankment?'

'I don't know . . . The only thing I can remember is that I was on my way back from Oss. And then . . .' She reflects for a moment. 'It suddenly got very misty. Yes, I remember now. I ended up at a roundabout and I couldn't read the signs. I must have taken a wrong turn.'

'But why were you driving so fast in the mist? That's not like you; you're always so careful.'

Senta looks at him in astonishment. 'Was I driving fast?'

'According to a witness, you were driving danger-ously fast, Mum,' Niels says. 'And that man should know: he saw everything.'

'If that man hadn't been walking his dog there
. . .' Frank shakes his head, as though wanting to
drive further thoughts away.

An uneasy feeling steals over Senta. It's as if
they're talking about a film they've all seen, one
in which she has the lead role, only she can't
remember any of it.

'What exactly happened?' she asks uncertainly.

'Can you really not remember, Mum?' Denise cries
out. 'You drove into the water! You nearly drowned!'

With a face that says he can hardly imagine
anything so horrific happening to his mother,
Jelmer sits up straight. 'That's so horrible,' he says
quietly.

Drowned. That's why she felt as if she had to
rise to the surface of the water. She'd driven into
the canal and almost drowned, and she can't
remember any of it.

'Who . . . how—'

'The man who saw it happen got you out,' Denise
says, helping her.

'I can't remember a thing. Not a thing.'

There's a short silence.

'It doesn't matter,' Frank finally reassures her.
'The most important thing is that you survived,
and that you escaped unharmed.'

They'll have to wait to see whether this is true,
and when their eyes meet they realise it

simultaneously. With the children there, they don't say anything more. She is alive, she has recognised her family, she can move and talk. The rest is for the future.

'I think you're better off not remembering,' Niels says. 'It'll probably save you a lot of nightmares. And then we'd have had to leave the lights on all night.'

Everyone laughs, even Senta. A few months ago they'd persuaded her to watch a horror film, and it had been weeks before she'd dared to go to sleep in the dark.

The atmosphere becomes more relaxed. The children all chatter at the same time, making jokes. Jelmer gets down from the bed and thoroughly investigates the catheter and the monitors next to the bed. Frank quickly takes the place next to Senta and strokes her hand again and again.

Senta doesn't say much. She looks, listens and enjoys. The visit from her family tires her out, but she'd rather bite her tongue than say anything.

Niels is right, she thinks. It's probably better that she can't remember anything about the accident; she doesn't want to end up with a lifelong trauma.

But this knowledge is shot through with something else: a nagging feeling that it *would* be better if she could remember the accident. And the reason why she was driving so fast.

21

Lisa answers the phone with an uncertain voice. 'Hi, Mum.'

'Hi, darling, it's me,' her mother says, rather unnecessarily. 'How are you doing?' Her voice sounds relaxed: she's clearly ready for a nice chat, and she has all the time in the world.

Lisa pictures her mother in the corner of her red sofa, a cup of tea within reach.

'Fine,' she says. 'Anouk is a bit ill.'

She doesn't know why she adds this; perhaps because it's what she normally would say. But a second later Lisa is ready to bite off her own tongue. Her mother immediately begins to ask worried questions and suggests coming round.

'Really, Mum, it's not that bad. But she's coughing, so I'm keeping her in as a precaution.'

Her mother has to agree that this is sensible. 'So

I don't need to come over? I don't mind at all, you know that. And you'll need to pop to the shops at some point.'

Lisa panics. 'Then I'll take her with me or leave her at home. She's old enough.'

'I don't agree, Lisa,' her mother argues. 'No one leaves a five-year-old at home, do they? You wouldn't really do that, would you?'

Under different circumstances, Lisa might have argued with her, just on principle, but now it seems better to give in quickly. 'No, I don't. You're right, Mum, anything could happen.'

Opposite her, Kreuger leans his arms on the table and gives her a broad grin. Lisa ignores him and half listens to her mother, who hasn't stopped talking.

'Maybe I'll drop by later in the week. Let's see. Or is Mark coming round?'

Lisa takes a deep breath and forces herself not to look at Kreuger. 'I don't know,' she says as nonchalantly as possible. 'He's very busy.'

'He has other commitments, you mean.' Her mother's voice suddenly sounds bitter, and Lisa knows what's coming.

'Mum, I have to hang up, I'm expecting someone. It's a mess here and I still have to do the washing-up—'

'Who's coming, then?'

'A friend of mine. You know her – Julia.'

'Oh,' her mother says disapprovingly. 'She's allowed to come round and your own mother—'

'I'm hanging up now,' Lisa says. 'I'll see you later in the week, all right? But give me a ring first.'

Her mother's exclamation that she wants to have a word with her granddaughter is cut off as Lisa hangs up.

Kreuger curses. 'Why did you hang up on her? You don't want that woman turning up here.'

Lisa reassures him that she has just ensured this won't happen: her mother and her friend Julia hate each other.

'And if she'd got Anouk on the line, she'd surely have slipped up.'

Kreuger thinks for a moment, but then nods in agreement. 'All right, well done.'

'I told you I'd play along.'

'Very sensible of you.'

'But what will I get in return?' Lisa wants to know, as if she's in any position to make demands. 'I mean, I'd like to know what's going to happen. How long are you going to stay here, do you think?'

'What do you mean? Are you fed up with me already?' Kreuger leans forward over the table. 'I'm disappointed in you, Lisa. I thought we were getting on nicely.'

'We are, but—'

Kreuger stands up in a flash and pulls Lisa from her chair. He is suddenly so terrifyingly close that she can see the bloodlust in his eyes.

'We are getting on nicely,' she says quickly. 'Really! I think we've got a lot in common. Don't we?'

If she hadn't been so scared it would have been fascinating to study the transformation in his bearing: from aggressive to somehow helpless.

'I loved her,' he says with difficulty. 'And you know, you look just like . . . you look just . . .'

To her dismay, Kreuger slowly brings his face towards hers. His mouth comes closer, much too close. His dark shaven head, the stubble on his chin, his spots, his greasy skin – they all fill her field of vision. His smell penetrates her nostrils and makes her feel sick.

Suddenly she feels his hands on her body. First only on her shoulders, but then they slide downwards in a single liquid movement to her breasts, where they rest for a moment before beginning a kneading motion.

It is though she's standing stark naked in her kitchen, instantly stripped of all feelings of self-worth. The adrenalin rushes through her body, spurring her on to push him away, to knee him in the crotch, to claw at his eyes.

Instead she remains motionless, frozen in

revulsion. Who'd have thought that she'd ever allow a stranger to put his hand down her top and get her breast out of her bra cup? At the same time she feels his other hand grab her behind and pull her to his crotch. His mouth descends to her neck before returning to hers.

Lisa clamps her lips shut reflexively, but he forces them open with his tongue, which he then sticks down her throat until she practically gags. Her entire body resists, and all of sudden she can no longer allow him to carry on.

'No!' she says with a strangled cry and pushes him off her.

He looks at her warily, like a predator wondering whether its prey really has the guts to fight back. 'What do you mean, no? Don't try to tell me you don't want it.'

'That . . . that's not it,' she says with difficulty. 'It's just . . . here in the kitchen, with Anouk so near by . . .'

There's a silence.

'I get it.' Kreuger's soothing tone makes it clear he's not angry. 'No problem. We'll just go upstairs.'

22

He places a chair under the bedroom doorhandle. To prevent Anouk unexpectedly coming in, he explains. He knows Lisa wouldn't like that. He always felt uncomfortable himself about his children catching him in the act.

Lisa doesn't dare look at the chair for long. Maybe she can toss it aside, pull open the door and run away.

And then? Kreuger is determined to have sex with her, and there is no escape. If she had any doubt about this, the erection, visible through the sturdy fabric of his jeans, dispels it.

What would happen if she resisted? He'd probably take it out on her struggling body, angered by her protests and tears. She can't afford to make this man angry.

Kreuger observes her from a few feet away. 'Take that top off, will you?'

Lisa doesn't move.

'Didn't you hear me? I said take that top off.' Kreuger sits down on the stool in front of her dressing table and waits.

The thought that he wants a striptease suddenly hits Lisa. Oh my God, this can't be happening . . .

She slowly pulls the white top over her head. She is wearing a T-shirt underneath it, which she also takes off slowly after a nod from Kreuger. Then she stands before him in her jeans and bra – a white lace bra that he appears to find very exciting. His mouth gapes slightly and a twinkle appears in his eyes.

'I think there are lovely tits under there,' he says softly.

She has to force herself not to cover herself up with her T-shirt. She drops it to resist the temptation.

Kreuger leans back. He doesn't seem about to approach her. Let's keep it like this: stay where you are.

'You must find yourself pretty,' he says. 'Especially when you walk round in a tight top and all the men stare at your tits. I'm sure you like that, don't you?'

'Yes,' Lisa confirms.

He doesn't have a reply to that.

'All women like to be looked at. It's a compliment,' she says in a defensive tone.

Kreuger's face suggests that her comment is a revelation to him. 'Yes, I guess so. They like that. Even if they get whistled at or are the butt of sexist jokes. They just walk on pretending to be annoyed, but deep in their hearts they like it. If you don't whistle at them, they're even offended. All women have double standards. There's no telling with them.'

Why are they having this conversation? Isn't he going to rape her? Did he just want to frighten her? No, his eyes are still fixed on her breasts.

Kreuger moves slowly towards her.

Lisa's mind races. 'Anouk was born in this room,' she says, nodding at the bed. 'It was a terrible birth. That's why we never had a second: I never wanted to go through that torture again.'

Lisa pretends not to notice Kreuger's frown. She lowers her voice as though sharing a deep secret. 'The midwife misjudged it. I should have gone to hospital, but we ran out of time. Luckily I didn't see the knife they cut me open with. But Mark did; he was standing next to me. He almost fainted. Can you imagine? They just chop your vagina open. And then they shoved in a vacuum pump and pulled out Anouk. We used to have a carpet, but we had to get rid of it. It was covered in blood.'

She looks at the floor, as though she can see through the laminate to the bloodstains below, and experiences the satisfaction of Kreuger's gaze also being pulled down.

'I could hardly walk for weeks,' Lisa tells him. 'Peeing was incredibly painful, and of course sex was out of the question. I had stitches everywhere. Mark didn't feel like having sex for ages either. He said: "Once you've seen a vagina in that state, lust abandons you."'

Kreuger's face contorts in disgust.

'How were your children's births?' Lisa inquires.

'Really easy. Angelique just shat them out and a week later we were having sex again.'

His body is closer now; she smells his sweat.

'Really?' Lisa takes a step back and leans against the door of the wardrobe. 'Life's not fair. Why should one woman suffer so much and another woman's children just pop out? But anyway, I'm just happy I live now. A lot of women used to die during labour.'

'Can't you shut up for two seconds?' He comes and stands right next to her, puts his hands on her breasts and squeezes.

Lisa inhales sharply. He seems to take this as a sign of pleasure, because he squeezes harder. Then he moves one hand to her buttocks and pulls her against him. She feels his cock growing and a wave of nausea washes over her.

'We're going to have a party together,' he whispers in her ear. 'You and me – how do you like that? I don't think you've been properly fucked for a good long time.'

His mouth descends to her right breast.

Lisa searches for a point somewhere above Kreuger's head and escapes outside – to the tops of the tall trees in the distance, their yellowing crowns rocking gently in the wind.

This isn't really happening, this isn't really happening, she repeats to herself like a mantra.

Kreuger detaches himself from her breast with a slurping sound and nods at the bed. 'Lie down,' he says.

23

Before the accident, Senta would often work at night; that way she could avoid being disturbed by ringing phones, colleagues coming in with questions, conversations going on around her. It was impossible to write her articles at work. She saved her creative energy for late in the evening, when the children were in bed and Frank slouched on the sofa watching a film. The night sheltered them then, formed a blanket around them.

But now there's nothing safe about the darkness that creeps towards her from the hall. She doesn't like the silence it brings either. She needs distraction, noises, voices – everything that prevents her consciousness from weakening and those unfathomable depths from opening up beneath her.

She knows that this is nonsense. Dr Reynders

has assured her that the test results were good. But fear prevents her from sleeping.

Senta turns her head to a stream of light that falls into her room from the corridor outside. She is tired, exhausted. After Frank and the children left, the tests continued. The entire evening. And now, now that she is finally alone with her thoughts, they flow over her like a waterfall.

'What can you remember from the day of your accident?' Dr Reynders had asked her.

She can remember everything, apart from the accident itself. The traffic jam on the way there, the idiot driver who'd hugged her bumper the whole time, her irritation. She'd deliberately slowed down, and when the man had tried to overtake her she'd accelerated, so that he became stuck in the queue in the slow lane. She'd seen in her rear-view mirror that the driver couldn't get back into the busy fast lane, and she remembered the contented feeling with which she'd driven on.

She had told Alexander and he'd laughed heartily. 'I always do that if someone's chasing me. Bait them a bit. I didn't know women did it too.'

Outraged by his sexist comment, she'd thrown the least dangerous object to hand, a banana, at his head. He had caught it laughing and pointed it at her like a pistol. 'Surrender or the punishment will be terrible!'

She had run away and he had chased her around the whole house, until their wrestling in the bedroom had turned into the best sex in ages.

She remembered all of it. Her feelings of shame, and the guilt when she drove off in her car, back to Frank and the children. She knew that her relationship with Alexander had to come out at some point, and each time she resolved to stop in order to prevent the major drama waiting for her. But each time she also knew she'd arrange to see him again.

In the beginning, she'd managed to keep her feelings for Alexander in check. After their first meeting, when they'd only kissed, she'd avoided further contact, afraid to start something over which she'd lose control. But, while she'd always given her life an eight out of ten, without Alexander it suddenly lost some of its shine, and she had trouble making a six of it.

Frank had noticed. Of course, he'd noticed; he knew her so well. After more than twenty years of marriage you no longer go weak at the knees with lust for your other half, but having sex once every three or four months was too infrequently. She didn't miss it, but Frank got grouchy.

Their relationship reached an all-time low one night when they were about to go to a party. She'd been wearing a new skirt with a low-cut top and a matching necklace, and had spent a lot of time styling her dark brown hair, which she'd put in rollers to add extra volume. Frank didn't like thick make-up and nor did she, but it had taken her at least a quarter of an hour to give herself a natural look. She'd come downstairs feeling really pleased with the results.

'Are you ready at last?' Frank said, picking up the festively wrapped bottle of wine from the table.

When he failed to compliment her, Senta walked past him into the sitting room and combed her fingers through her thick dark hair. 'Wow, Senta, you look nice,' she said.

Something in her voice made Frank look up and she glared at him accusingly. 'Do you realise you never pay me any compliments? You never say that I look nice.'

'You always look nice.'

'But it's sometimes nice to be told!'

Frank looked back at her with a twinkle of amusement in his eyes. 'Wow, sweetheart, don't you look nice.'

She shrugged resentfully, went into the hall and put on her coat.

'What? Now I give you a compliment and it's all wrong!'

'You should work on your spontaneity,' Senta snapped.

'If I don't pay you a compliment, you complain that I never pay you a compliment; and then when I do pay you a compliment, you complain that I can't be spontaneous any more. What do you want?'

'Boy oh boy,' Senta replied irritatedly. 'As far as you're concerned I could go around in dungarees and a bowl-cut.'

'You'd be just as pretty,' he said sweetly.

He meant well. That was the problem – he meant everything well, but he couldn't sense what was missing in their relationship. And what was missing was the spark that prevented this kind of argument from happening in the first place.

It's strange to have lost a part of your memory. Even though it was a small part, it was still the most crucial moment of her life. She could have died. She'd thought she was going to drown, and experienced panic and mortal terror. Or had she lost consciousness immediately and been oblivious to the car filling with water and sinking? Is that the reason why she can't remember the accident?

The idea of a sinking car makes Senta shudder. Niels was right: she should be thankful she can't remember anything.

Did Alexander know she was in hospital? There's no telephone in her room, and her mobile is irretrievably lost. Senta forces herself to think. Of course, there's an advantage to this: no one can one can pick up her voicemail or read her text messages. She is surprised when she realises that she still knows Alexander's number off by heart.

Tomorrow she'll ask Frank to buy her a new mobile phone. As sleep slowly engulfs her, the bitter irony of this plan hits home.

24

Lisa can't get to the bed: her legs are too weak to control. His saliva burns on her breast, and her knees have almost given way.

'Don't be nervous. You'll enjoy it.'

He tugs her away from the cupboard and pushes her towards the bed. At the same time he fumbles with the zipper of his jeans.

'Undress,' he says, repeating his command.

If she wants to survive, there's only one choice, but dear God!

Weary with misery, Lisa sinks on to the bed and lies on her back.

'Open your trousers,' he says, as he lets his own drop.

She doesn't get much further than opening her zip. She can't bring herself to pull down her trousers.

Kreuger kicks off his shoes with a couple of rapid movements and steps out of his jeans. His legs are skinny and covered in black hairs, and his underpants need a wash.

Lisa quickly looks at something else: the watercolour of a tropical beach hanging on her wall. The mattress creaks; he's beside her. Out of the corner of her eye, she can see him looking down at her, supported on one elbow. He traces the curve from her breast to her navel with a finger.

'Take off your trousers,' he says softly.

Her eyes become damp, but she stops herself from crying. She can't turn into a sobbing wreck. Crying women bring out the worst in men, reminding them of their vulnerability and reinforcing their conviction that they can do what they want with them.

With great difficulty, she wriggles out of her skinny jeans. Kreuger pulls off her shoes and throws them to the ground. The jeans follow.

'So,' he says as his eyes travel over her body. 'It would be nice if you didn't look so frightened. Am I that disgusting?'

The threat in his voice quickly causes Lisa to shake her head.

'Is it such a punishment to have sex with me?' He becomes even more threatening, and again she shakes her head.

'My hand,' she says weakly. 'I hurt my hand.'

With an expression that suggests he'd forgotten the violent start to things, he looks at the bandage: a new red stain is showing through. His face relaxes, becoming almost friendly.

'All right, I was afraid you were taking the mickey. I mean, I feel something between us. Something very special. Don't you?'

She nods wordlessly, and he bends towards her, kissing her on the mouth. 'So, try and be sweet to me.'

His hand slides into her panties and his fingers begin to search.

Lisa opens her lips. Her body shakes heavily, like the onset of an epileptic fit.

'That's nice, isn't it?' Kreuger says with a smile as he pushes his fingers in. 'Now then, darling, now you can do something for me.'

Full of disgust, Lisa rubs his back with the palm of her hand, as though her fingertips were too sensitive to bear contact with his skin.

'Is that all you can come up with?' he says with irritation.

She swallows with difficulty. 'Calm down, we've got lots of time.'

Terrifying images in which she is forced to cater to all of his needs appear in her mind's eye, but it soon becomes clear that he doesn't have that much self-control. If she's clever, she can make sure he's satisfied before she has to work through an extended programme.

Rather more motivated now, she strokes his back and his biceps, and lets her hand slide into his underpants. She tells herself to hurry.

Her hand reaches for his cock and begins to work it. Kreuger withdraws his fingers from her and lets out a panting groan. 'Oh my God, that's fantastic.'

He attacks her breasts, biting and lapping at them. Lisa turns her head away and looks out of the window. Just a little longer and she'll be done with it.

'Spread your legs,' Kreuger gasps as he pulls down her panties. He moves upwards and forces his tongue into her mouth. Feeling as if she's choking, Lisa suffers what Kreuger undoubtedly takes for a passionate kiss. He frees his penis from her hand, pushes her legs open and bores into her.

Hammering and jerking, he works himself up to a climax, but the time it takes seems endless.

The tropical beach, with its palm trees and intense blue sea, looks reassuringly peaceful. Years ago, before Anouk was born, she and Mark had gone on holiday to the Dominican Republic. They'd taken a diving course in the hotel swimming pool. Lisa will never forget her first experience of sinking down into the under-water world of the Caribbean Sea with an oxygen tank on her back. The multi-coloured coral reefs, the schools of tropical fish and the gentle blue of the water formed a fairytale world. Her eyes, like one of the sponges she touched with her fingertips, soaked up all the beautiful things around her, storing this peaceful world some-where deep in her heart so that she could return to it whenever she wanted. Like now.

Her gaze becomes hazy and she breathes more and more shallowly, until everything seems to move in slow motion. The groaning and panting above her takes on a dull sound and a mantra hammers away in her head, cutting through the pain and disgust. *I'm not here, I'm not here, I'm not here.*

Her soul takes a step back and moves to a world that no noise can penetrate, where every movement is slow and gentle. An aquamarine, swishing under-water world in which schools of tropical fish swim around her and waving plants caress her body. Lisa is safe under water, and when Kreuger is finally done with her, she has to try very hard before she can surface again.

25

Someone has come in. Far away in her dreams, Senta hears the rattling of a trolley and the muted chatter of nurses in the corridor. She slowly leaves the dream world where she is roaming about in the fog and returns to reality.

There's a light on in the glass-enclosed nurses' station. Senta's monitors give off some light, but around her bed it is dark. She hears the beeping of the equipment around her.

Senta forces her eyes shut. For reasons she doesn't understand, she wants to return to her dream. She doesn't know exactly what it was about – the images have vanished – but the uneasy feeling she'd had has not dissipated. The many invisible threads of her mind hold on to it tightly, as though trying their best to attract her attention.

Hospital life slowly starts up, making it unlikely

that she'll be able to fall asleep and return to her dream. Finally, Senta accepts that the day has begun.

'Good morning!' Dr Reynders stands at the foot of her bed, smiling. 'How are you feeling today? Sleep well?'

Senta smiles back. 'Yes, very well. I had some confusing dreams, but I feel rested.'

'Fantastic.' Dr Reynders looks at her chart. 'I've got good news. The most recent tests were all excellent. I think we'll be able to discharge you soon.'

'I can go home? When?'

'Let's see.' Dr Reynders sits down on a stool next to Senta's bed. 'Victims of near-drowning who haven't inhaled water can usually go after a day, but you lost consciousness. According to your rescuer, you lost consciousness just before he got you above water. He felt you go limp. The second you lose consciousness, your mouth opens and water pours into your lungs. We couldn't detect any, but even a minute amount is enough to cause ARDS.'

'ARDS?'

'Acute Respiratory Distress Syndrome: a dangerous reaction to injury or infection that can manifest itself up to forty-eight hours after a near-drowning. The chance of its happening now is small, but I'd rather keep you in an extra day.' Dr Reynders gives Senta a searching look. 'How's your memory now? You still don't remember anything of the accident?'

'No, nothing at all.'

'Hmmm, then the likelihood of its returning is quite remote. Not that that matters, you know,' she adds hastily. 'It's very common for accident victims to forget the circumstances after a hard knock or oxygen deprivation. Some people lose a few minutes, some an hour or more. We call it retrograde amnesia.'

'So I've lost that hour for ever?'

'It's possible,' Dr Reynders says, nodding. 'But if you think how lucky you are to have survived unharmed, I wouldn't worry too much about it.'

'No,' Senta agrees. But after the doctor gives her a firm handshake before continuing on her rounds, she spends a long time staring at the ceiling.

In the afternoon she's transferred to medium care. When Frank arrives, she's just been moved into a room with three other patients.

'It was quite a hunt finding you!' He's arrived with a broad grin, a bunch of flowers and a few magazines. He bends over Senta and kisses her on the lips. 'Hello, darling, how are you feeling?'

'Good, actually. I'd like to go home.' She accepts

the magazines and buries her nose in the flowers. They are sunflowers, fresh and cheerful, with thick stems. 'How beautiful! Thank you. These will brighten up this boring room.'

'And afterwards you can take them home with you.' Frank sits next to her on the bed and Senta moves over to give him more room. He wraps an arm around her and pulls her close. They sit like this for some time, not saying a word.

Finally Frank breaks the silence, his voice a little hoarse. 'Jesus, Senta, I really thought I'd lost you.'

'Yes . . .' she says quietly.

'I've spent a lot of time thinking. About you and me, about our relationship, our family, how we'd talk the day over, just the two of us, with a glass of wine in the evening . . .' He twists a piece of Senta's hair around his finger, an old habit he'd abandoned years earlier. That glass of wine had become less frequent recently. She understands what he means: that he too is aware that something in their relationship has imperceptibly changed.

'I'd thought the children had grown so much, but suddenly they were really . . . childish,' Frank says. 'One minute they're all gobby, and the next all three of them are pressed against you crying.' He stops, stares into the distance and then gives her a sideways look. 'This could have been the end of our family. Of my life. If you'd drowned, it would have ruined my life, Senta.'

His voice sounds serious and so open. All of a sudden she has a crystal-clear recollection of the moment she fell in love with him. They had both been studying at the School for Journalism. From the start they'd been in the same circle of friends; they had often worked together and helped each other with their essays. But no sparks flew until a party, just before graduation. Up to that point she'd considered Frank a nice boy, a good friend, but nothing more. But at the party she'd become aware for the first time of how cheerful he was; he was always so full of stories. Frank livened up any group of people he joined. He certainly wasn't the most handsome man at the school, but he always knew how to draw the attention of the female students. That evening he'd seemed quite intimate with Miriam, a girl that Senta didn't know well. She saw them standing there, their arms wrapped around each other, the besotted look Miriam gave him, and she felt a fierce stab of jealousy. She realised she wanted Frank herself, and she made sure that she got him. She seduced him. Frank didn't know what had hit him, but he went along with it without reservation. He dropped Miriam like a hot coal, and when he took Senta back to her student flat that evening, he admitted that he'd had an enormous crush on her all through college. He'd never admitted it because he didn't want to ruin their friendship.

That Senta seemed to reciprocate his feelings made him unspeakably happy.

'What are you thinking?' Frank's mouth is right next to her ear.

'About that party and our first kiss.'

Frank smiles at the memory. 'The best night of my life. I can remember every hour of that evening, you know? My life didn't really start until then.'

It sounds dramatic, but Senta knows that she's always been the centre of Frank's world, and even though she's started to take this position for granted, she's never doubted his love for her.

'You should make sure you love your husband less than he loves you,' her mother used to say. 'Otherwise you'll feel dependent and unhappy and no man is worth that.'

What her mother hadn't said was how tiring it was to swing constantly between periods of doubt and certainty.

'How have you managed at home?' she asks now. 'Nijmegen is quite a long drive.'

'We're staying at Anka's. She wants to come to see you.' Frank gives her an understanding look.

'Not right now. I only want to see you and the children for the time being.' Senta doesn't feel like the company of her boisterous cousin, or that of any other family member. 'Have you told my father?' she suddenly asks.

'No, I thought I'd wait. Given his heart problems. You agree, don't you?'

'Yes, of course.'

Frank gets down from the bed and gives her a kiss. 'I must go. I'll come back this evening with the children. Do you need anything?'

'Yes.' Senta hardly dares look at him. 'Could you get me a new mobile phone?'

26

It feels like she's been crying for hours, gently and soundlessly. Kreuger has gone downstairs. He'd smiled at her from the doorway, and she'd been able to muster just enough strength to smile back at him. After that she'd lain there completely frozen for minutes, staring, as though by not moving the terrible thing that had happened to her could be undone, or in any case ignored. But the anaesthesia that had been keeping her emotions under control slowly began to wear off, and the tears came with the unstoppable force of a tidal wave. They rushed over her, and she pressed her face into the pillow to stifle her sobs.

Kreuger had stripped a layer from her; he had roughly torn away the shield that had provided her with protection and self-confidence, a vulnerable but, until now, untouched second skin of self-esteem and identity, leaving her soul exposed and bare.

Lisa turns on to her side with a groan, and suddenly realises that Anouk is alone downstairs with Kreuger. She gets up in a panic and dresses. However much she'd love to spend hours in the shower, she has to make do with clean clothing.

As she walks down the stairs with difficulty, a nagging pain between her legs, she continues to repeat to herself that this isn't the end of her life. She is still breathing, she is still the same Lisa that she was an hour ago. And, at the same time, she realises what a ridiculous thought this is. Nothing will be the same from now on.

If he has done anything to my daughter, I'll murder him, she thinks grimly. I don't care what the consequences are; he'll pay with his life.

She pushes the door handle downwards and almost throws open the door, afraid of what she will see. Her gaze darts first to the dining table, which is covered with open pots of finger-paint and sheets of Anouk's artwork.

Where is Anouk? She hurries inside and looks wildly around her.

'Anouk!' she cries with a catch in her voice.

'I'm in the kitchen, Mummy,' comes her daughter's voice.

Lisa hurries to the kitchen. Anouk is standing on a chair by the worktop and washing her hands carefully with soap, assisted by Kreuger. 'Good girl, and now that bit. Look, your thumb is still red.'

Lisa leans against the doorpost and takes a few deep breaths. Her heart begins to beat calmly again, and she manages to put on a smile when Kreuger looks around at her.

'She made a lot of paintings,' he says cheerfully.

'I saw. Lovely!' Lisa's voice sounds strange, and her smile feels like a plastic mask on her face, but Kreuger doesn't seem to notice. He looks satisfied, relaxed even, until Anouk jumps down from the chair and runs to her mother, as though she can't take another minute of Kreuger's company. With a wild gesture, she throws her arms around Lisa's waist and presses her face against her.

'Where were you?'

'I had to do something upstairs. You were having a nice time painting, weren't you?'

'You mustn't go away. Why wouldn't the door open?'

Oh my God, she tried to come in, Lisa thinks in a flash. Her eyes find Kreuger's over the top of her daughter's head, and suddenly she feels almost grateful to him for having secured the door; he had spared Anouk something, at least. If that had indeed been his intention, and he hadn't just been trying to stop Lisa from making a speedy escape. It's hard to see inside the mind of a killer, a child killer at that. Perhaps the deranged mind that caused him to commit such horrendous deeds also contains some humanity. She has to trust that this is the case. He hasn't murdered them, and it doesn't seem like he is planning to, although she can never be sure. She hasn't got a clue what his next move might be.

Her injured hand has stopped throbbing, and she spends the rest of the afternoon in the kitchen. She has always enjoyed cooking, and it is her saving grace now. It gives her something to do, distracts her from her fears. She fetches the radio from the basement and turns it on low, so as not to disturb Kreuger, who is watching sports in the sitting room. He has got a bottle of beer from the garage and put his feet up on the coffee table. If she didn't know better, she'd think it was Mark sitting there.

Her eyes glide to the photos attached to the fridge with magnets. Lots of pictures of Mark and herself, moments from another life, when they'd only just met and she was still young and full of hope. Convinced of her attractiveness, sure of her power to get him, exclusively, for herself alone.

She opens the door of the microwave to check whether the meat has defrosted yet. She has always filled her cupboards and freezer with tins, bread and meat, to cut down on shopping trips. Given

Anouk's attacks of breathlessness, she'd done a huge shop on Saturday.

Perhaps it would have been better if the cupboards had been bare today. But Kreuger would probably have ordered in pizza. Or, more likely, they'd have lived on stale bread and leftovers.

The least she can do is to continue to take good care of herself and Anouk, to keep up her strength. She might desperately need it.

It is as though she has been sucked out of her normal life and spat out into another dimension. Over and over again, her troubled soul projects images in her mind, like a faulty video camera playing on a loop.

Lisa gets the meat from the microwave and puts it on a chopping board. Lean braising steak, or 'stewed meat', as she always called it. It was her favourite dish as a child. She didn't have much of an appetite as an adolescent, but whenever her mother cooked stewed meat, Lisa would devour it. It was the first dish she learned to make when she left home, and she still found it delicious.

She puts the braising pan on the stove and adds a chunk of butter. When it has turned brown, she lays in the strips of beef. The meat singes with a hiss. A few cloves, a couple of bay leaves and chopped onion. A delicious smell drifts through the kitchen, the smell of the past, of her home. An overwhelming feeling of homesickness comes over her. She forces herself to hum along to a song on the radio, but she can't stop her tears from adding themselves to the gravy.

27

Lisa spends another night in the basement with Anouk, but when Kreuger lets them out the next morning there's a change in his attitude. He stands there almost awkwardly, but doesn't go so far as to apologise. To Lisa's amazement he has laid the breakfast table, and the coffee is already brewed. She sits down wondering what will happen next.

Anouk can feel the change of atmosphere and gives her mother a questioning look. When Kreuger's attention is elsewhere, Lisa shrugs.

They eat without saying much, apart from a few comments about the warm weather. And then, completely out of the blue, Kreuger says, 'If I asked you to go with me, what would you say?'

The question falls into the room like a stone breaking through a window-pane. Lisa looks up, perplexed. The spoon she is using dangles in the air like an exclamation mark.

'Go with you? Away from here, you mean?' she asks cautiously, as though his suggestion might have other meanings.

Kreuger takes a sip of coffee and nods. 'Would you come?'

Lisa's brain works at top speed. She silences Anouk with a glance and answers as coolly as possible, 'Who knows?'

Kreuger adds a second spoonful of sugar to his coffee and stirs it brusquely. 'Or would you run away as soon as you got the chance?'

'I haven't run away in the past two days.' Lisa forces herself to take a bite of bread, to chew it calmly and to swallow before she continues. 'This is my house, and I consider you a guest here. It's true you forced yourself on us, but in the end we've got along quite well, don't you think? You promised me that you wouldn't harm us, and I took you at your word. Why would I run away?'

He studies her for a long time, but she continues to drink her coffee and to return his gaze. When the silence continues, she casually asks him where he might go.

'I've got family in Germany,' Kreuger replies.

Lisa nods approvingly. 'Germany is a big country.'

'Even in a small country they can't find me,' Kreuger says with a grin.

Anouk looks from one of them to the other and sprinkles icing sugar on her rusk.

'The police are looking for a man on his own, not a man with a woman and a child,' Lisa says. 'We could take my car. We'd be over the border in a jiffy.'

She finds it difficult to hide her tension. She'd do anything to get him out of the house. Once outside, there would surely be a moment when she could try to escape. A sudden swing of the wheel and a minor traffic accident would be enough; or she could drop notes out of the car window, or shout for help at a petrol station. Enough possibilities.

'Hmm, maybe it would be better just to stay here.' Kreuger empties his coffee cup with a few large gulps. 'But I could do with your car.'

'Take it,' Lisa offers. Hope darts through her: maybe he's thinking of leaving very soon. Who knows, perhaps this nightmare will be over right after breakfast. 'I've still got a few of Mark's clothes. We could bleach your hair to make you unrecognisable.'

He gives her a brooding look. She takes a small mouthful of bread to gain some time. However hard she tries to swallow, it remains a sticky ball in her mouth. Finally she washes it down with a large gulp of coffee. 'You think I'll tell the police.'

'I don't think it, I know it,' Kreuger says calmly.

'Maybe you're wrong.'

'But it's not a chance I can take. You must understand that?'

Her armpits begin to sweat and her hands feel clammy. What is he trying to tell her?

'Once you've gone . . .' she says, carefully formulating her thoughts, 'they wouldn't be able to catch you right away. If I went to the police, you could take revenge.'

'That would be possible,' Kreuger confirms.

'And if they never caught you, I'd spend the rest of my life being afraid. I don't fancy that. I just want to be able to leave the house again, to get on with my life. And I want to remember you as an unexpected guest I came to an agreement with.' She holds his gaze. 'The agreement that I won't betray you.'

The silence between them is explosive.

'Hmm,' Kreuger finally says. 'But there's another possibility: I could just take Anouk with me.'

28

'I've got more good news for you.' Dr Reynders enters Senta's room in high spirits. 'I think we can release you tomorrow. You suffered a concussion when you hit your head on the steering wheel, but we don't need to keep you in for it. I was concerned about the risks of a lung infection, but it looks like you didn't swallow any water.'

A broad smile travels across Senta's face. 'That's certainly good news.' Then relief is replaced by worry. 'Has the risk of infection disappeared completely?'

'I wouldn't let you leave otherwise. But I'll give you some antibiotics as a precaution, and paracetamol for your headache. How is that now, by the way?'

'Not too bad,' Senta quickly reassures her. She isn't going to let a headache keep her in hospital.

'Great. Just take things easy at first, that's my recommendation.' Dr Reynders gives Senta a warm look and carries on with her rounds.

When she's alone again, Senta takes a deep breath. Luckily she can go home. She is totally fed up with watching television and leafing through magazines. Which she takes as a good sign. If it's up to her, she'll resume normal life again as quickly as possible.

Her new mobile, a trendy pink model, is lying on her bed, shining at her seductively, but she hasn't yet gathered up the courage to use it. Yes, she called her father, who is in a nursing home. But she hasn't yet dialled that one number, the one constantly running through her head.

Senta looks at the phone in indecision.

Does Alexander know she's in hospital? It's possible. Frank had told the magazine about the accident and, given that the sound recordings from the interview have been lost, one of her colleagues should have let Alexander know that the article would be delayed.

Alexander . . . She'd like nothing better than for him to turn up and take her in his arms. But a small, barely identifiable change has taken place inside her, and it is making her hesitate before contacting him. If anything has become clear during the time she was unconscious, it is that Frank and the children form the core of her existence. Knowing this, she should put an end to her relationship with Alexander, instead of indecisively staring at her new mobile. This is a good time to start again, to stop lying and deceiving, and to leave that nagging guilty feeling behind. But then she'd also have to say goodbye to something that gives her days a little more shine, that makes her blood quicken, and removes years from her age. She might have forgotten the accident, but she has held on to the amazing feeling she had on Monday after leaving Alexander's house and saved it in every cell of her body. She had no idea that he'd become so important to her. It's a disturbing thought that she's let things go too far.

Senta hesitantly reaches out her hand and picks up her mobile. Then she makes a decision and quickly taps in the number. Her heart skips a beat when she hears Alexander's deep, powerful voice.

'It's me,' she says. 'Senta.'

There's a short pause and then he says with surprise, 'Senta, how nice of you to call.'

Nice of her to call? He should be delighted. In the background she hears the rattle of a printer and automatically asks whether it's a good time for him.

'Fine, yes, not a problem. That's to say, I was busy, but I don't mind your calling. You know that. I was just surprised that I didn't recognise the number.'

'I've got a different phone. My old one got wet. I'm in hospital, Alex.'

'In hospital? What happened?' he asks in a concerned tone.

'I drove my car into a canal.'

Alexander inhales in shock on the other end of the line. 'My God,' he says once he's recovered himself. 'What happened?'

'I can't remember. I must have hit my head on the wheel. I've got bruises on my forehead and concussion. But I can't remember how it happened, or how I got out of the car. I didn't swallow any water, so I must have come to after the impact and held my breath. If I'd remained unconscious, I'd have got water in my lungs. I know that at a certain point I was helped out of the car. Someone jumped into the water and pulled me to the surface. The car was at the bottom by then.'

'My God,' Alexander repeats. He sounds deeply impressed. 'Have you spoken to him or her?'

'It was a man, and no, I haven't spoken to him. But I'm going to get in touch with him.'

'It's a miracle you survived. Do you know when you can go home?'

'Probably tomorrow. They're keeping me in today just to make sure I don't develop an infection.'

'ARDS,' Alexander says knowledgeably. 'That is indeed something to worry about.'

'Apparently the chances aren't that great any more. So I'm allowed to go home.'

'Are you allowed any visitors before then?'

'Frank and the children are here as often as possible.'

There's a pause, then Alexander says gently, 'If I could, I'd jump in the car right away and come to you. You know that, don't you?'

'Yes . . .'

'If there's anything I can do for you, just say.'

'Think about me a lot. Cross your fingers that I don't get an infection.'

'I'd do that anyway. And I always think about you a lot. I love you.'

Senta smiles, but then a nurse comes in and she jumps. 'I've got to hang up.'

'Take care. I'll call you.'

29

Lisa comes within a hair's breadth of letting her coffee cup slip through her hands. 'No,' she says firmly. 'Out of the question.'

It clearly amuses Kreuger that she thinks she's in a position to forbid him anything. His laugh resounds through the room.

Lisa remains resolute and continues to reason with him. 'What would you do with a small child? She'll only make things difficult for you. She's ill, she'll cry, she'll attract attention. No, you'd be better off going on your own. I'll give you everything you need: my car, money, clothes, food, just name it. We can even drive to the bank; I've got quite a lot in my account.'

'That's awfully kind of you,' Kreuger says with a deadpan expression. 'Really awfully kind.'

Is he mocking her? Lisa picks uncertainly at her

placemat. She might be better off shutting up now, before she comes across as too anxious. She's made a suggestion, and every word she adds is one too many. If she could only work out what he's thinking.

Kreuger has laid his arms on the table and looks out of the window, sunk in thought. Lisa gets up without making a sound.

'Mummy, can I play on the computer?' Anouk asks.

Lisa looks at Kreuger, and he nods.

Anouk jumps up from her chair happily and waits until Lisa has started up the computer. The machine quickly buzzes to life and connects with the outside world. Everything in Lisa is tensed. She takes plates, cutlery and glasses to the kitchen and sets them on the worktop. Then she opens the dishwasher, gets out yesterday's clean wash and puts it away. In the meantime, she listens tensely to the computer's sounds. She knows she can't just sit down and send an email. But Anouk knows how to open Outlook Express. Anouk could send an email; she writes to her father sometimes. Why hadn't she thought of that sooner?

Her head pounding, Lisa puts the breakfast things in the dishwasher. Can she risk asking her daughter to do something so dangerous? Or is he testing them?

She calms down immediately. Of course it's a test. Kreuger had children that age himself; he knows the computer skills that Anouk would have by now. Maybe he's waiting for her, Lisa, to make an attempt to send an email. If he leaves them alone in a minute's time, it will be because he wants to spy on them.

She gets up and closes the dishwasher. With a dustpan and brush, she clears the crumbs from the kitchen floor and throws them in the bin.

When she goes into the sitting room, Kreuger has gone. Lisa pricks up her ears and hears him pulling the toilet roll in the bathroom. He stays away for so long that she becomes sure he's putting on a show.

She walks to the cupboard in the hall with a stoical face, gets out the vacuum cleaner and sets to work. The temptation is enormous, but she cannot take the risk. Not now that he's on the point of leaving.

She is given lots of opportunities to raise the alarm throughout the day. The computer remains on, and Kreuger regularly leaves her alone downstairs. When she goes upstairs to fetch the dirty sheets, she suddenly sees her mobile lying on the bed.

Lisa stands motionless, prey to torturous indecision. All her survival instincts scream at her to pick up the telephone and dial 112. She doesn't have to give a detailed explanation; just a few seconds would be enough. But what if this is another test? Maybe Kreuger has put her mobile on the bed in such a way as to alert him if it's touched. She'd have to put it back in exactly the same place. Perhaps he's put a hair on it, or devised some other cunning trick. Or is she thinking too much?

The phone lies on the cheerful floral duvet cover, screaming for her attention. Lisa starts to sweat. Apart from her mistrust, there's another emotion at work: fear. It paralyses her muscles, makes her ears roar and her hands shake. She looks nervously over her shoulder. Where is Kreuger now? She left him downstairs, but he's probably just at the bottom of the stairs. Maybe he's removed her SIM card.

She doesn't do it. Her mobile is lying there too obviously, too nonchalantly. Kreuger must have put it there deliberately.

But this does give her the opportunity to write a note to the postman.

She hastily searches Anouk's room for a sheet of drawing paper and scrawls her cry for help in red felt-tip pen with lots of exclamation marks.

Please help me! The escaped criminal Mick Kreuger is holding me and my daughter hostage! This is NO joke! Please take this note to the police at once!

Lisa Fresen

She tears off the bottom part of the sheet, folds the written part twice and puts it in her jeans pocket. Then she gets the washing basket from the bathroom and goes downstairs, her body shaking. Her cheeks are burning when she enters the sitting room.

Kreuger is sitting in front of the television, zapping through the 24-hour news headlines. He gives her one very brief glance. Lisa ignores him. She walks to the washing machine in the utility room and sorts through the laundry. She takes her time and gradually calms down.

You haven't done anything, she reassures herself. He can't accuse you of anything. You didn't take the risk and that was very sensible.

The problem is that it doesn't *feel* sensible. She never would have thought she'd behave so passively in a threatening situation.

'You didn't have a choice,' she mutters. 'It would be different without Anouk, but you simply don't have a choice now.'

She gets up and suddenly Kreuger is standing behind her. Lisa cries out in shock.

'Don't be afraid!' He puts his hands on her shoulders, and Lisa knows that he can feel her shaking. 'Hey? Are you so frightened? I just wanted to tell you something.' He waits a while and then gently squeezes her shoulders. 'You won't sleep in the basement tonight,' he says, with the expression of someone offering her a magnificent gift.

'Anouk can return to her own room, and you too. With me,' he adds.

Hope and a sense of resignation make way for a new feeling of horror. Lisa desperately tries to adopt a pose she can hide behind, but she fears he can see right through her. His sardonic laugh confirms this, and so does the hand on her buttocks.

'I'll leave at the end of the week. Sunday evening I think.' Kreuger grabs her backside more firmly. 'But I won't take either of you with me. That would make things too complicated. We'll say goodbye for good on Sunday. So we'll just have to enjoy ourselves for the rest of the week, don't you agree?'

30

Alexander phones in the evening, after visiting hours. This time he wants a detailed account of everything she can remember and what she experienced during the coma.

'Were you really completely absent or did anything get through?' he asks with interest.

'You know, it was just like I was swimming around in a deep dark sea,' Senta says pensively. 'Unfathomable depths that pulled me down like a magnet. Sometimes I managed to get to the surface and then I heard people talking, and was aware of my surroundings. I knew I had to come out, but I just couldn't. I kept being pulled back down into the depths. It was very frightening.'

'Could you hear the doctors? What did they say exactly?'

Senta tells the story, interrupted by Alexander's

questions from time to time. His interest does her good, and she talks ten to the dozen about everything that she remembers from those lonely hours.

When she finally hangs up, she's exhausted, but she still has difficulty in falling asleep. Alexander's detailed questions have made her restless. Frank didn't ask her nearly as much, for fear that he'd tire her out or that she'd get upset. His eyes told her again and again that he could barely believe that the catastrophe threatening them had been averted.

Senta turns on to her side and sighs. There's something wrong, but she doesn't know exactly what it is. Only once she's dozed off and has reached a state between waking and sleep does the answer come to her.

31

The mattresses are back where they belong: in Anouk's room and in the spare bedroom. Anouk is happy, but Lisa would have preferred to stay in the basement. It is Wednesday evening, and even if Kreuger does leave on Sunday, he's got four long nights to enact all of his sexual fantasies with her.

I have to get away, she thinks feverishly. If *he* doesn't leave, I will. *With* Anouk.

Tonight seems like the best time to escape. She can try to get away when he's asleep.

The whole evening she keeps a discreet eye on Kreuger. Her mobile has disappeared from her bed. He must have put it away somewhere. It might be in his trouser pocket, along with the keys to the front door and her car. Or has he hidden those too? That would make matters rather more complicated. They'd have to escape through Anouk's bedroom window. She pictures herself edging down the drainpipe to the garage roof with a frightened, trembling child. She'd have no hesitation in doing it on her own, but can she force Anouk to attempt something so dangerous?

She doesn't have a choice. She can't imagine Kreuger simply leaving them behind when he goes on Sunday. However sympathetic he might seem at the moment, he's still a criminal, a murderer with a diminished sense of moral responsibility. Since she started to cooperate, he has changed, but she can't count on the change being a permanent one. He might have planned it all this way. She cooks for him, does the washing and lets him fuck her. He couldn't have found a better deal. But she won't find out what his real plans are until Sunday.

Lisa stares out of the window with her arms folded. She's going to do it. Tonight she'll climb out of the window with Anouk.

When she puts her daughter to bed, she dresses her in warm flannel pyjamas and sets her hoody apart from the rest of the clothes in the wardrobe. She'll be able to grab it easily tonight. She puts out Anouk's trainers and looks around. Does she need anything else?

A rope around her waist, she thinks. A rope to bind her to me in case she slips.

A feeling of desperation comes over her and she sinks on to the edge of Anouk's bed.

'What's the matter, Mummy?' Anouk asks sleepily. 'Why were you getting my hoody?'

'Oh, no reason,' Lisa says. 'Go to sleep. Isn't it lovely to be back in your own bed?'

Anouk rolls on to her side. 'When's he going away?' she mutters drowsily.

'Soon,' Lisa promises her with a kiss on the cheek. Very soon, she adds to herself.

His arm is wrapped around her like a tight chain. Lisa has turned on to her side with her back to him and stares into the darkness. Her nakedness screams out at her, accentuated by Kreuger's hand, which has been on her right breast for more than an hour now. Her body is sore where he has bitten her. She has endured it again, relieved that the darkness could hide her tears.

Her throat is fighting against the bile that keeps rising from her stomach. If she's not careful, she'll wake him up by vomiting. Is he really asleep? She keeps her eyes constantly on the red digital numbers lighting up her bedside table. An hour and a half already. She listens to his breathing – calm and regular. His grip on her breast has weakened. That could mean he's asleep. Or he could be pretending.

A new wave of nausea wells up in her. To the

bathroom, quick. She worms her way out of Kreuger's grasp and slides out of bed. There's a strong smell of sex and sweat all around her. No wonder she feels sick.

She starts to feel better as soon as she's on the landing. She takes a few deep breaths in relief and goes to the bathroom to take a sip of water. It stays quiet in the bedroom. Is he really sleeping deeply? She listens carefully, but can hear only his regular breathing. It's such a relief just to be away from him for a while that she can't bring herself to return to the bedroom.

But she needs clothes, even if it's only her dressing gown. It's risky, but she'll have to search his trouser pockets to see if he has her mobile or keys. Probably not, but you never know. It might spare them a dangerous escapade on the garage roof.

Lisa looks at herself in the mirror. Moonlight falls through the window and lights up her pale, waxen face. There are circles under her eyes, and her hair hangs flat and lifeless around her face. A shadow of the woman who unsuspectingly hung out the washing on Monday afternoon.

She tries to encourage herself. Go on, girl. Tiptoe into the bedroom and quickly check his trouser pockets. A piece of cake.

She's trembling too much to walk on tiptoe. She shuffles back to the bedroom, one foot in front of the other, into the darkness and the stench. Kreuger is snoring lightly.

Lisa silently walks around the bed to where his clothes are messily piled on a chair. Her hands are shaking, her wound suddenly throbbing, as she feels around until she finds the tough denim of his jeans. If there are keys in the pocket, they might clink.

She picks them up very carefully. Her fingers find his belt and then slide around to the pockets. They are disappointingly light. She cautiously slips her hand into the first pocket, but it is empty.

Kreuger turns on to his side with a groan. Lisa's nausea returns at full force. She can't vomit, not now. She breathes deeply in and out, and when the wave has subsided a little, she hurries her hand into the other pocket. It too is empty. She had expected this, but the disappointment is still harsh. Nothing for it now but to get Anouk on to the garage roof, only she doesn't know if she'll manage with her legs feeling so weak.

Her eyes slide to the empty place next to Kreuger in the bed, and her face contorts into a grimace. Of course she'll manage. The alternative is unbearable.

She picks up her dressing gown, which is lying at the foot of the bed, and takes it with her. She puts it on outside on the landing. She is suddenly angry with herself for not having any trainers, only shoes and high-heeled boots. They would make much too much noise, and might easily cause her to slip on the sloping roof. It'll have to be bare feet.

Wake up Anouk and get her into her hoody. Hope that she doesn't protest at the top of her voice or insist on going to the loo.

Lisa creeps to her daughter's room, but then the bile rises again unstoppably. A few more steps and she's in the bathroom, where she collapses on to her knees in front of the toilet bowl.

Her stomach heaves, her body cramps, and she feels it coming. Her vomit hits the water in the toilet. So much noise. She isn't surprised when she hears someone coming into the bathroom behind her.

'What's the matter with you?' Kreuger's voice asks.

She doesn't go to the trouble to answer, but holds her long hair into a ponytail with one hand. Every time she stops to catch her breath, her body shakes and she starts to gag again.

Kreuger watches her from the edge of the bath. Lisa ignores him.

When she's got to the point of vomiting only water and bile and her body has regained its composure, it occurs to her that tomorrow she'll have to spend another day and another night with this man. She wipes her mouth, takes the beaker of water that Kreuger offers her with her shoulders slumped and begins to cry. Kreuger soothingly strokes her hair.

'Poor Lisa,' he says. 'Poor, poor Lisa.'

32

The first thing she sees when she parks in front of the door are the streamers. Pink, blue and white, they are draped around the door, across the front of the house, along the garden fence all the way to the street. If they'd had enough streamers, they'd have included the lamp-post, Frank tells her.

Senta gets out of the car, her eyes damp. She can hardly control her emotions when she sees her children waiting for her in the sitting room full of flowers. They burst into cheers and throw themselves at her; even Niels wraps his arms around her and presses his cheek against his mother's in a silent display of affection.

'Oh, children, how lovely.' Senta cuddles each of them in turn.

'We've got cake too!' Jelmer cries, and pulls her with one hand towards the kitchen, where an enormous iced chocolate cake is waiting on the worktop. 'This is your favourite kind of cake, isn't it, Mummy?'

'Absolutely.' Senta reassures him. She turns to Frank, who is watching her every movement, his hands in his pockets and a wide grin on his face. A wave of tenderness and devotion runs through her. She walks over to him and kisses him gently on the lips.

'Thank you,' she says quietly. 'What a wonderful homecoming.'

'You should thank the children: they dreamed everything up.'

'But it was your idea to—' Jelmer begins, but he is attacked from all sides before he can finish his sentence.

'That's a surprise, you idiot,' Denise says.

This earns her a kick, but Jelmer's happiness at having his mother home again is too great for his humour to be spoiled.

'When are you going to do the surprise, Dad?' he whispers into his father's ear, very loudly.

'In a minute.' Frank gives him a blatant wink.

'I'm starting to get curious. What's going to happen?' Senta looks from one person to the next with interest.

'You'll see!' Jelmer dances around excitedly. 'It begins with a—'

'Jelmer!' Denise presses her hand against her brother's mouth. 'Shut up. It's not the same if Mum already knows. Mum, go and sit down; we'll bring you a cup of coffee. Or would you rather have tea? And would you like a big slice of cake or an enormous slice of cake?'

Senta says she'd prefer coffee, and a medium-sized piece of cake. She lets them lead her to the sofa as if she's an elderly lady who can hardly walk. Home. At least her brain is telling her that this is home, but she somehow feels estranged from all the familiar things around her. She is constantly aware that she almost lost her family, her home and her life. If that man hadn't been walking his dog along the embankment, she'd be in a coffin now. No streamers, no cake, but deep mourning in this house. She shivers and dismisses such macabre thoughts.

And suddenly, as she tries to turn her mind to a happier subject, something flashes through her mind.

A house, she thinks in surprise. I dreamed about a house.

The big surprise is a new car: a metallic silver Toyota Auris Business Edition, only a year old. Frank enthusiastically demonstrates all the extras, and hopes that Senta will take it for a test drive immediately.

She imagines putting on the seat belt, turning on the engine, driving away. She turns pale and brings her hand to her forehead. 'I think I'll go and lie down. I'm shattered.'

'Of course, darling. I totally forgot how tired you still must be. You go and lie down. I'll get dinner ready for tonight. We'll have a lovely long one, glass of wine, music . . .' Frank solicitously leads her inside, and upstairs, to bed. The children follow, watching her go and waving goodbye before disappearing into their bedrooms or off to see their friends.

Frank unpacks her suitcase and helps her on with her nightdress. 'Are you all right like that?' He looks concerned as she crawls under the duvet.

'Yes, thanks. You're such a sweetheart.'

'Sleep well, darling.' He gives her a quick kiss and leaves the bedroom, closing the door softly behind him. 'Don't play your music too loud, Mummy's sleeping,' Senta hears him say to one of the children.

But she isn't sleeping and she isn't planning to. All she wants to do is to lie quietly on her back, stare at the white ceiling and enjoy the peace. But wherever she looks, that house appears in her mind's eye. Is it a memory? Something from that lost hour? But why does she remember a house and not the moment she drove into the water?

Senta stares ahead. It was a misty afternoon, and she was lost. The only thing she can think is that she asked for directions somewhere. Maybe she sat in that house for a while until the mist lifted; maybe she had a drink and a nice chat with whoever lived there. Maybe he was the one who rescued her from the water.

Senta jumps up with a start. Her saviour! Of course, he saw everything happen; he'll be able to fill in a few missing pieces of the puzzle.

Sleep is out of the question. She throws off the duvet, pulls on her dressing gown and goes downstairs. A strong oniony smell meets her, and Frank looks up in surprise.

'Couldn't you sleep?'

'No, I'm too restless. I suddenly thought about that man who rescued me. Do you know who he was?'

'Yes, I wrote it down. I imagined you might want to thank him. And the police said it's sometimes good if the victim and the rescuer get to know one another. It helps you to process things.'

'It might get my memory working again. That missing chunk is bothering me.'

'Yes, I'm sure. People might say that an hour isn't important, but the hour before something so fundamental . . . I'd like to know what happened too.' He skilfully turns over the onions in the pan.

'Where is that man's number?' Senta asks.

'I wrote it down in my diary. It's next to the computer. But Senta . . .' He looks up with a light frown between his eyebrows. 'Do you really have to call him now? You've only just got home.'

'I'll just copy it down. I'll call him during the week. Maybe he wouldn't mind my dropping round.'

Frank points the knife at her in warning. 'You know you're not allowed to drive yet.'

'Who said so?' Senta gives him an astonished look. 'I'm absolutely fine. Why shouldn't I drive? You wanted me to go for a test drive just now.'

'With me next to you! What if you blacked out?'

'Why would I black out? Did Dr Reynders say that might happen?'

'No, but you never know.'

'Oh . . .' Senta scratches her cheek thoughtfully. 'Let's see: when *do* you think I'll be capable of going out on my own?'

Frank turns to her with a sigh. 'Don't be so sarcastic, Senta. I'm worried – you must be able to understand that?'

His shoulders slump, and suddenly he looks so tired and worn out that Senta goes over to him, full of remorse, and wraps her arms around him. 'I'm sorry, you're right. I'd be worried too if it had been you. But, to be honest, I can't wait to get back to work and on with my life again.'

'You mean carry on as though nothing has happened?'

'Yes, that too.' Senta stops talking for a moment and then continues in a gentle voice. 'I'm afraid that if I wait too long I won't dare to.'

Frank's eyes are serious and full of understanding. 'A week of rest isn't too much to ask, is it? Really, Senta, you owe it to yourself to let your body heal. It's been through a lot.'

Senta nods in acquiescence.

That evening they share a Mexican meal, which Frank has cooked. Burritos, nachos, guacamole, her favourite foods. Frank hasn't skimped on a thing. The good Chilean wine on the table completes the picture, and Niels and Denise are allowed a glass each. Only Jelmer has to make do with a Coke, but he doesn't have a problem with that.

'Wine is disgusting, I don't know why you like it.'

His father nods approvingly. 'Keep it that way.'

'I don't like it that much either,' Denise admits after a tiny sip. 'It's so sour. Haven't you got any sweet wine?'

'Get yourself a Coke too,' Senta advises her. 'I don't really approve of your drinking alcohol. Before you know it, you'll start to like it.'

'Yes, and then you'll be just as addicted as Mummy and Daddy,' Jelmer says between bites of his burrito.

Senta and Frank both look up speechlessly and then say at the same time, 'Hang on!'

'You drink wine every evening with dinner,' Jelmer says accusingly.

'Having a few glasses with a meal won't do any harm,' Frank replies calmly. 'But it can damage children whose brains are still growing. That's the difference.'

'Give Jelmer a glass, then. He hasn't got a brain to grow.' Niels taps against his brother's head, at which Jelmer pelts him with the brown beans that have fallen from his burrito.

Denise bursts out laughing, but Frank puts a stop to the chaos with an angry outburst.

'Oi! Stop it! Your mother has only been out of hospital for a few hours and you've already started playing up!'

The children look in Senta's direction in shock, but she's laughing behind her napkin.

'I'm so happy to be home again,' she says.

The rest of the evening is peaceful and convivial. No one is withdrawn or absent; they all gather together in the sitting room like a model family, chatting and reading. The television is on, but it's more of an unobtrusive murmur in the background. When the eight o'clock news starts, Frank immediately turns from his family and gives it his full attention. Senta is forced to follow the summary of the world's woes along with him. She is not happy, but she knows that Frank likes to watch the news for work. After a while, her thoughts wander off and she watches without really seeing anything.

'Haven't they caught that loony yet?' Niels says. 'It's unbelievable.'

'He's long over the border,' Frank comments. 'They won't be able to catch him any more.'

Senta absent-mindedly looks at the image of a man with short black hair and a round, surly face that fills the screen.

'An escaped nutcase,' Niels fills her in. 'He escaped while on day-release from a psychiatric prison, killed a woman and beat a man to death.'

'What a creep.' Senta is watching the screen with only half an eye. She isn't really following the news item about the criminal, but when the coverage changes to the weather, she experiences a strange sense of relief.

33

Lisa slowly opens her eyes. She has spent the entire night awake. Kreuger's slightest movement in the bed sent shockwaves through her body; every time he snored or groaned in his sleep she'd freeze, and when his hand brushed her body it felt like he'd touched a raw nerve.

The relief when he finally got up in the morning and left her to doze was like a painkilling infusion into her veins. Still, she must get up; Anouk would be awake soon.

Just as she's stretching her limbs, her daughter comes through the door. Anouk glides in and climbs into bed with her. Her daughter dozes off, and Lisa softly strokes her dark hair. She stares blindly at a chink in the curtains and at the daylight streaming in. Had things had gone differently, they would have been safe in a police station by now. Or Kreuger would have been arrested straight away, in the night, and they'd have the house to themselves again. Will she ever be able to live in this house again as she used to? If she does stay here, she's going to throw away everything Kreuger touched, starting with this bed.

But thinking about the future is a luxury she cannot permit herself as long as they remain in this nightmare. She's not even sure she has a future.

The sound of heavy footsteps on the stairs. Lisa jumps out of bed on an impulse, until she realises she's naked. She quickly gets back under the duvet.

Kreuger's tall shape fills the doorway. 'Do you feel any better?'

You could read the frown on his face as concern, but Lisa hears the undertone of irritation in his voice.

'Yes,' she says submissively.

'Not feeling sick any more?'

'No, I'm all right now.'

'Have a shower,' Kreuger advises her. 'It stinks like hell in here.'

He turns around, and she hears him going back downstairs. Slowly, so as not to wake Anouk, she sits up and pushes off the duvet. A shower, that's a good idea. Although it might be better to go down with stinking breath and bits of vomit in her hair. Nevertheless, she turns on the shower. Soon the warm stream is washing away the previous night. But only once she's soaped herself from head to toe and washed her hair three times does she feel any better.

She returns to the bedroom with a hand towel wrapped around her body and looks in her wardrobe. A baggy grey cardigan and a worn-out pair of jeans look like a suitable choice.

'Has he gone, Mum?' Anouk sits up sleepily.

Lisa is startled out of her thoughts. 'No, he's downstairs.'

'Oh.' Anouk goes barefoot to the bathroom.

'Why are we allowed in our own beds again?' Anouk asks when she returns.

'I don't know exactly. I think he wants to be friends with us.'

Anouk peers thoughtfully into the large mirror on the wardrobe. She goes to her own room and returns with a pink tiara in her uncombed hair.

'I don't want to be friends with him,' she says resolutely, as though she's been considering it and has now made her decision.

'No, me neither.' Lisa pulls her daughter towards her and gives her a cuddle. 'But we need to pretend. You know that, don't you?'

'I know. But sometimes it's hard.'

'I know. But you . . .' Lisa is about to begin a

serious conversation with her daughter when the landline rings somewhere in the house.

Suddenly alert, they look at each other, and Lisa thinks how absurd it is to have a five-year-old child as an ally.

The ring sounds muffled, as though it's coming from inside a cupboard. She hears Kreuger moving downstairs, walking through the sitting room and into the hall. A key is turned in a lock and the ringing becomes clearer.

So the phone is in the hall cupboard or in the meter cupboard.

Lisa waits anxiously for Kreuger to tell her to come downstairs and answer it. But before this can happen, the ringing stops and silence resumes.

She hurries downstairs, expecting the caller to try again.

'Who was it?' she dares to ask.

'Mark.' Kreuger puts the phone in his trouser pocket and goes back into the sitting room.

Lisa's mouth has become dry. She isn't religious, but she is praying feverishly that he'll call back. He is harder to fob off than her mother. Mark isn't exactly the patient type, and if he wants to speak to her he'll keep trying until he gets hold of her.

In the kitchen, she takes cheese, butter and bread from the fridge.

'Was that Daddy?' Anouk asks in a penetrating whisper.

Lisa nods and puts her finger in front of her lips.

Anouk sits down at the kitchen table. 'I was supposed to be going to the zoo with Daddy.'

Lisa tries to keep Kreuger in her line of vision through the half-open door, but he's out of sight. She turns to the worktop with a sigh and grates some cheese for Anouk's sandwich.

The telephone rings again and she jumps, causing the grater to slip. Holding a bloody thumb in her mouth, she waits tensely, but Kreuger doesn't call her. He just lets the phone ring, until the answering machine kicks in.

A familiar voice resounds through the house, one that fills Lisa's eyes with tears.

'It's me.' She hears him hesitate. 'I wanted to call you sooner, but I was just too busy. I want to arrange a time to take Anouk to the zoo.' Silence. 'I miss you, Lisa. I hope you've changed your mind. Monique knows about us now. I told her. She wants a divorce, Lisa.'

Another silence, then a click announcing that the caller has hung up. His final words pulsate through Lisa's head, as a deadly silence descends.

She stands frozen at the worktop, her thumb still in her mouth, her eyes focused on the door. Anouk, who started off looking happy at the sound of her father's voice, now looks hesitant, as though she can sense danger. There's no movement from the sitting room, until heavy steps come towards the kitchen. An ominously heavy tread, as though Kreuger's repressed anger is being expressed through his feet.

One step to the side is enough to give Lisa a view of the sitting room. And of Kreuger just outside the kitchen door.

34

She pulls Anouk towards the utility room.

The door to the basement is open, and the key is still in the lock – she saw it there last night and vaguely wondered if she could hide in the basement in an emergency. It would have to be a real emergency, because they'd be caught like rats in a trap.

This thought screams in her head as she sends Anouk down. But she has no choice. The moment Kreuger enters the kitchen she grabs the key from the door and goes through it.

She slams it behind her and turns the key. A grey darkness encompasses them. A scrap of daylight breaks through the high window, lighting up a spot on the concrete floor.

She is still standing at the top of the stairs when Kreuger throws himself at the door. 'Open up!' he shouts. 'Open up, you filthy bitch!'

Lisa sees Anouk put her fingers in her ears in the half-light. Her whole body is shaking. She pulls her daughter towards her.

'I knew it!' Kreuger screams. 'You're no better than all those other bitches with their filthy lies! When I get my hands on you, I'm going to cut off your tits and strangle you with your bra!'

His shoulder rams the door, but the heavy wood resists his attack. Lisa and Anouk hurry down the stairs, arms wrapped around each other, and wait.

'Mummy . . .'

'Shh, now, he can't get to us.' Lisa's voice is trembling.

The banging and swearing carry on for a while but then suddenly it goes quiet. To her frustration, Lisa can't hear a single sound that might tell her what Kreuger is planning. Nailing the door shut? Lighting a fire? Oh God, please no.

In the hours that follow, she hears his heavy footsteps above their heads, and now and then water rushes down the pipes that run through the basement. They hear him come into the utility room and stand in front of the basement door a number of times. Then she holds her breath and waits for the sound of a crowbar or a saw. But Kreuger doesn't seem to be going down that route. He just leaves them in the basement, and Lisa understands why: there is no food here, nothing to drink and no bedding. They can spend the night on the cushions from the garden chairs, but that's about it. It wouldn't be so bad if they had any water. They can cope for a while without food. But how long can a person survive without fluids?

She hunts through the space yet again, in the hope of finding a forgotten can of cola or a bottle of water, or even a bottle of wine. She used to keep her supplies here, until she took a tumble down the steep staircase and broke her ankle. After that she moved everything into the utility room and the garage. She didn't have much reason to go down into the cellar, especially once Mark began to view the basement as his DIY space. He liked to make things, but there was no place to work in his own house, which lacked a cellar or a garage. He'd even repaired and repainted a second-hand bike as a birthday gift for his elder son under her roof.

With painful sharpness she remembers the day she discovered how close hatred and love were to each other – the day she realised that her own fantasies had begun to lead a life of their own and to create their own reality.

Only part of Mark belonged to her; the other part would always be inseparably bound to his wife, Monique. Lisa had done her best not to become emotionally dependent on Mark, but on the day she realised that he wouldn't leave his wife for her she felt as though a meteorite had smashed into her world.

A few weeks after they met, he told her he was married and that his wife was pregnant. Lisa could understand why he wouldn't want to abandon Monique when she was expecting his child. So for the first few months after Sam was born, she didn't insist that he leave Monique. He spent every free moment with Lisa, and they lamented the fact that they hadn't met a year earlier. She had really believed they had a future together, and still believed it when Sam turned one. But when Monique became pregnant again, Lisa began to have her doubts. She raged at Mark. How could he have been so stupid as to have let this happen? Was she supposed to sit out another pregnancy and the baby years of their second child before he'd leave his wife? She had lost faith in him, and, despite all of Mark's pleas and assurances that he was serious about her, Lisa had ended their relationship.

She'd cried herself to sleep for nights on end but held firm: she never wanted to see Mark again.

Then he sent her two gifts: one package contained a blue Babygro and the other a pink one. He wanted to have a child with her, he'd written on the card – proof that he was choosing her, not his family.

'If you leave your family now, you're an even bigger prick than I thought,' she wrote back. 'My children deserve more than that – and I do too.'

Not long afterwards she found out she was pregnant.

Contrary to what she had told Kreuger, the period following Anouk's birth was amazingly joyful. The birth had been fast and easy; she'd not had post-natal depression, and she'd walked on clouds for weeks. And Mark had been at her side, as radiant as she was.

'Thank you, thank you,' he'd repeat while kissing Anouk's black hair. 'I already had two sons and now you've given me a daughter. Isn't she beautiful, Lisa! Just look at her!'

She had looked at her baby, and then at Mark, and she'd seen his deep love for her and Anouk through his eyes. And they had made up.

'I'll leave Monique,' he had promised her. 'Our marriage isn't important; it never has been. Not since I met you. I'm so fed up with all the arguments and her possessiveness. Please be patient, Lisa. I have to find the right moment to tell her. It's not a small matter, and I also have to think about Sam and Tim.'

Lisa understood this and gave him time. But when she celebrated Anouk's first birthday, there was still no change in sight.

Anouk was eighteen months old when Lisa unexpectedly ran into Mark with his family. That experience made Kreuger's story horribly familiar: the
desperation, the wild jealousy and the hatred that
had surfaced in him when he saw his ex-wife with
another man; the irresistible urge to take revenge,
to kill. But, while he had acted on his feelings, she
had put on an inner brake. At the very last moment,
it has to be said.

She was waiting at the traffic lights in her car
when she suddenly saw them. They were coming
around the corner, the elder boy skipping ahead,
the younger in the buggy. They didn't look like
they had marital problems. On the contrary: their
faces were happy, and they were talking and
laughing. And they kissed just in front of Lisa's
nose, before going in different directions. Monique
went into the toy shop with the children, and Mark
hurried to the newsagent's on the other side of the
road.

He stepped out into the road and looked back
over his shoulder to shout something to his wife.
Monique smiled, gave him a thumbs-up and blew
him an air kiss.

And that's when Lisa released the brake. The
traffic light was on green now, and the driver next
to her was revving his engine aggressively.

If she'd stepped on the pedal with all the

intensity of her feelings, Mark would have been under her car two seconds later. The temptation was enormous.

That's it for you, she thought.

But she had held her foot poised above the accelerator and hesitated – an instant of rationality that had saved Mark's life, one that she was thankful for much later. The rage, though, had flooded through her body for days, turning into bitter, deep regret shortly afterwards.

On that day, she'd ended their relationship again, afraid of the intensity of her feelings and the unpredictability of her moods.

35

Senta had imagined that being back home would be rather different from this. She wanders restlessly through the sitting room, a cup of coffee in her hand. She has a long afternoon ahead of her, hours to kill with nothing but her own thoughts. If it had been up to her, she'd have returned to work. She'd soon know if she wasn't up to it. What's the point of hanging around the house all day? Work is no punishment for her; it's what she likes to do best. What's more it would be a distraction from all that pointless worrying about the accident and how close she'd come to death. One shouldn't dwell on things like that.

She puts down her coffee mug on a pile of Denise's exercise books and sits at the piano. They both play the piano, but Senta has hardly touched it in recent years. She tinkles the first notes of 'Für

Elise' with one hand, but has forgotten the rest. A few years ago she could play the whole piece effortlessly.

Her eyes glide over to the silver photo frames displayed on top of the piano – pictures of the children when they were still sweet little toddlers. How big they have become. Their rounded cheeks have become thinner, their eyes less curious and open. In the photos she takes now, they always look like they are suffering slightly, as if they are only posing to make her happy.

A feeling of nostalgia overwhelms her, even though she knows this is ridiculous. If you want the past back, you have to accept all of it, including the sleepless nights and the lack of time for yourself.

Things are fine as they are, she decides. She is happy with her life, her work and her freedom. She is even able to look forward to the time when it is just her and Frank in the house again, and they can go on the round-the-world trip they've always talked about.

Her thoughts instantly move on to Alexander, as though his name is inextricably linked to Frank's. To her surprise, she doesn't feel that familiar sense of loss. What was recently a welcome addition to her life is now mainly a complication that she'd miss like she'd miss toothache. How could she have found her life boring? How could she have thought that her work, husband and children weren't enough to make her happy?

Senta tinkles away at the piano some more, but soon stops. It is a beautiful autumn day. Frank had dutifully kept her company the whole morning. He looked up in concern every time she took a step, or yawned, or made the slightest sound, as though she might collapse at any moment, frothing at the mouth. He finds it hard to believe that she can't remember anything of her suffocating adventure under water, and he has taken Dr Reynder's warning that a lung infection could still develop very seriously indeed.

An emergency call from the newspaper presented him with huge dilemma. Could he go to the office and leave his wife alone?

'Go on, I'll manage,' Senta had said. 'Really, if bubbles start coming out of my mouth, I'll call you.'

He couldn't help but laugh. 'You'll call 112 right away. Have you got your mobile in your pocket? Good. Keep it with you; don't leave it lying around.'

'I will. Bye, darling.' Senta kissed her husband and then went to the window to wave goodbye.

She'd remained standing there long after the sound of the car's engine had died away. The children were at school, and a pleasant peace had descended on the house.

But after a half hour of reading magazines, answering emails and calling her father, the quiet had begun to get on her nerves. She was rarely home alone, and on the occasions when she was, she was always working.

Senta leaves the piano, picks up her coffee from the exercise book and gulps it down. Then she goes to her study and searches through the mess on her desk for the piece of paper with her rescuer's contact details. She finds it quickly, not yet buried under all her other papers.

'Rob Wenteling,' she reads aloud. His address and phone number are written underneath.

She picks up the phone and calls him.

'Rob Wenteling speaking.'

'Good afternoon, this is Senta van Dijk.' Her legs suddenly feel weak and she sinks down on to the desk chair. 'I'm calling to thank you.'

There is a pause and then Rob Wenteling says, 'You're the woman who drove into the water.'

'Yes. And you got me out. I'm really incredibly grateful to you.'

Rob Wenteling dismisses this at once. 'Anyone would have done the same. How are you getting on?'

'I got out of hospital yesterday. That was pretty quick, given the circumstances. I've been very lucky.'

'That's for sure!'

They discuss Senta's health briefly, and then she asks him whether he'll be home this afternoon. Rob Wenteling says that he will; he's retired and has a lot of free time.

'Can I drop by and thank you in person? And would you show me the site of the accident? I still can't really remember what happened,' Senta says.

Mr Wenteling hesitates, then agrees to her visit and offers to go with her. 'I can show you exactly where it happened.'

'Fantastic, thank you.' Senta looks at her watch. 'It will take me an hour or two to get to you.'

'I'll be waiting for you,' comes the simple response before they hang up.

Filled with new energy, Senta gathers her things together. It's difficult, because she has lost so much. It'll be a while before she can get a new driving licence. But, because she has a spare credit card that she usually keeps in her desk, she'll be able to fill up the car without any trouble and buy a large bunch of flowers for her rescuer.

Soon she is sitting at the wheel of her new car, somewhat awkwardly, studying the dashboard. It doesn't seem to offer any insurmountable problems. It's a Friday afternoon; the roads are still quiet; she'll figure out where all the knobs are while she's driving. She experiences a short burst of fear, but when she switches on the engine and moves out of the drive, it fades away. The Toyota Auris is obedient and practically noiseless. What a lovely car! It's like flying. Senta drives down the road filled with joy.

She is about to turn left on to the ring road, when she changes her mind and drives towards the shopping centre. She parks and hurries to the shops. She picks up a large bouquet of flowers at the florist's, a good bottle of wine at the off-licence and then, at the last moment, goes into Halfords and buys a LifeHammer. Fluorescent yellow, so that she can see it in the dark.

Back in the car, she puts the flowers and the wine on the back seat and unpacks the LifeHammer. She puts it in her coat pocket, starts the engine and glides out of the parking space.

She knows she must relax. She turns on the radio and sings along to the latest hits, which she knows off by heart because Denise and Niels play them at full blast every day. But whenever water shines in the distance she stops singing and slows down. She keeps a very close eye on the oncoming traffic and the cars behind her, wary of unexpected manoeuvres. She is relieved when a crash barrier looms up next to her and accompanies her for part of the journey. Whenever the waterfront pops up treacherously, her hands grip the steering wheel hard, turning her knuckles white.

Calm down, she tells herself. You're not driving fast, and there isn't a soul on the road; you won't drive into the water. And this time, if it does happen, you've got a LifeHammer. One tap on the glass and you'll be out.

Still, she doesn't breathe properly again until the motorway winds away and there is no more water to be seen.

36

They spend the entire afternoon sitting on the floor on the cushions from the garden furniture, and then spend the night on them too. No blankets – just arms around each other. Anouk doesn't complain once. She puts up with the hunger, thirst and discomfort with a composure far beyond her years.

'If Daddy comes, he'll send the bad man away, won't he?' There's such hopeful expectation in Anouk's eyes. Lisa doesn't have the heart to take this from her.

'Of course,' she says. At the same time, the thought that Mark is sure to come by tomorrow adds to her panic. How will Kreuger react?

'I'm cold,' Anouk admits miserably.

Lisa pulls her close. This child has given her so much joy. Even though life hasn't gone the way she'd planned, it has at least given her Anouk.

What did he say on the answering machine? That he is going to divorce Monique? Hope, mixed with a fear that she'll have to go through everything she's already had to bear all over again, overwhelms her. She leans against the wall, her eyes closed, Anouk in her arms.

37

'Here is where it happened.' Rob Wenteling points at the water flowing quietly past. The sun is shining; the surface of the water glistens, reflecting the reeds and the blue sky. An unthreatening beauty spot in the Gelderland countryside.

Senta stands up to her ankles in the long grass and has trouble imagining that she fought for her life here. In her mind's eye she descends to the bottom of the canal and shivers.

'Are you OK?' Rob asks, his voice full of concern. When they had introduced themselves and she had given him the flowers and the wine, he'd still been a stranger to her, but after she'd heard the short version of the story of how he'd rescued her, it had been difficult to stay formal.

'In some cultures, rescuer and casualty maintain

a spiritual connection for ever,' he had said. 'Even blood ties can't compete.'

This is undoubtedly true. Even if she never sees this man again, she'll think about him for the rest of her life.

'Yes, I'm fine,' she says when she realises that Rob is looking at her searchingly.

Rob Wenteling is a calm, dignified old man who looks older than he is. After retiring, he gave up his daily shave. He has a grey beard and large, bristly eyebrows.

'The village children think I'm Father Christmas,' he had said with a smile.

Senta could imagine that.

After they'd had coffee, they'd gone to the site of the accident. Wolf, the sheepdog who had been with Rob on the Monday, walked alongside them off the lead.

'You came from this direction.' Rob gestures to the left, where the road bends away from them a few times. 'I heard you coming and I thought, they're going fast. I went to stand on the verge and called Wolf. You drove past, probably didn't even see me in the mist, and then suddenly I heard the screech of your tyres. I began to run at once, but you'd gone into the water quite a way off. When I got there, the car had already disappeared under water. It was a while before I could find the right place. At last I saw the brake marks on the road and the tyre imprints in the grass. I kicked off my shoes, called 112 on my mobile and dived into the water.'

They remain silent, their eyes fixed on the same spot.

'And then?' Senta asks finally.

Rob Wenteling tells her. How scarily dark it was under water. He had concentrated on the car, which he could see only because the headlights were still burning. It was sinking quickly. While he was diving, they suddenly went out. Rob had cursed inwardly and immediately begun to doubt the location.

Descending to the bottom with powerful strokes, he arrived just as the car landed with a bump.

It was so dark down there, he told her, that he was unable to see what he was doing. He had swum around the car and let his hand glide over its side, looking for the door handle. But the only thing he could feel was glass. He kept reaching and searching, and then his head began to pound. Despite this, he continued, and suddenly his fingers closed around the edge of a door. It was slightly ajar. He somehow managed to pull it wide open and to feel around in the space inside, until his hand brushed against something heavy that was hanging half out of the car. A woman's body.

To his relief she moved when he pulled. If she had still been in the seatbelt, he'd have had a problem.

It wasn't difficult to get her out of the car: under water the weight of the body didn't play a part, but he had become desperate for air. With one arm around her waist, he worked his way back up to the surface of the water.

The journey upwards had seemed interminable. His lungs ran out of oxygen, and he came up panting for breath. Using his single free arm, he made his way to the bank with awkward strokes. He grabbed hold of a clump of reeds with one hand and pulled himself up. It cost him all his strength to pull Senta's limp, heavy body behind him. He wrestled his way along, pulling and tugging, and when they were finally on the bank, he fell to the ground next to her body. He wheezed and hacked, but every second counted. All the time they'd been under water she'd worked along with him, but just as they'd surfaced her body had gone slack. Despite his exhaustion he began mouth-to-mouth at once.

'So I wasn't unconscious for long,' Senta says.

'No, not under water, but once you were up I couldn't get you to come round. I carried on breathing into you; I was afraid I'd have to give you cardiac massage. Luckily you suddenly began to breathe again on your own, but you remained unconscious. I stayed with you and kept an eye on your breathing until the ambulance came,' Rob recounts.

Overwhelmed by his story, Senta throws both her arms around him. Rob lays a comforting hand on her shoulder.

38

As Senta drives back along the embankment, she is troubled by the thought that she will probably never see Rob Wenteling again. Everything that had to be said has been said, but she is still saddened to be leaving him behind.

She turns left, the direction in which she was going when the accident occurred, and follows the curves of the bank at a steady speed. Why on earth was she driving so fast on that particular afternoon? She hates mist and drives carefully in it. Why wasn't she doing so on that day?

The only thing she has to go on is a certain feeling, which she is sure is somehow connected with the house she keeps picturing.

Her mobile rings. As she's getting it out of her jacket, she sees that it's Alexander calling. Her instinct is to answer straight away, but she has a sudden image of herself speeding over the bank of the canal while she fiddles with her phone. She calmly pulls over before answering.

'I'm in the car,' she says without any preamble.

'In the car? So soon?' Alexander's voice sounds surprised and worried.

'Don't worry, I'm fine. I went to the place where the accident happened.'

'Oh!' He sounds even more surprised. 'How was it?'

'Strange. I couldn't really imagine it. If it wasn't for the brake marks on the road, it would look just like any other spot.'

'How can you be so sure that it was the right place, then?'

'I called the man who rescued me. We went to the site together, and he told me his side of the story. I was really lucky, Alexander. Unbelievably lucky. I wouldn't have survived without Rob's help, that much was clear.'

'Did you remember anything new?'

'No, I didn't. Only just now, when you called, I had a flash of myself driving along the embankment while I was doing something with my mobile, and at that moment I felt a real sense of urgency.'

'Like you were in a hurry,' Alexander says.

'Could something have happened? I mean, *before* the accident?'

'Maybe. I keep imagining a house. I'm going to follow the embankment to see if I can find it.'

'Can you wait for me? I'd really like to go with you,' Alexander says.

'Then I'd have to sit here for three quarters of an hour!'

'OK, OK,' Alexander says quickly. 'Tell me more about that conversation with your rescuer. What was he doing on the embankment, what did he see, what did he do when . . .'

Senta looks out of the window. A few ducks are chasing each other, flapping and quacking across the water.

'It was misty . . .' she begins slowly. As Senta recounts the story, she keeps getting the feeling that Alexander isn't really listening, that he's doing something else. She hears the tap of a keyboard and stops abruptly.

'What are you doing?'

'What?'

'You're taking notes. You're typing.'

From the hesitation in his voice, she knows that she's right.

'Have you got over your writer's block?' she inquires.

He laughs affectedly, expectantly.

'You're not listening to me properly.'

'Senta, that's not true. I'm listening really carefully to you.'

'You're listening, but not to me. You're listening to your character.'

Alexander sighs deeply. 'Senta, you have to understand—'

'Are you using this for your book?'

He is quiet for a moment. He is about to speak but Senta interrupts him. 'I'd rather you didn't call me again.'

'You don't mean that! Senta, please, I—'

'A few things have become clear to me over the last few days, Alexander. And one of them is that I love my husband – too much to keep doing this to him. I should have made the decision earlier, but the old Senta wasn't capable of it. The new one is.'

She hears him suck in his breath. 'Senta—'

'Good luck with your book,' she says gently. Then she hangs up and stares into the distance for a long time.

39

Is he still in the house? It wouldn't be all that surprising if Kreuger had just slipped off and left them in the basement. Each time Lisa thinks he has finally gone her cautious hope is shattered. The sound of footsteps or of running water whenever he has a shower betrays his continued presence. A short while ago she heard the familiar rumble of the post van and the crunch of the postman's foot-steps on the gravel. It struck her that perhaps she could open the high window in the basement and drop her SOS note through the narrow opening. She could just reach it, standing on a stool. But would it help her? There is no reason for anyone to come to this side of the house.

At least as long as she's locked up here, they are no longer exposed to Kreuger's violence and sexual impulses.

Lisa forces herself to push away thoughts of those repulsive moments. If she allows herself to think about being raped, she knows she'll break down. Every time the images rear up in her, she forces them back into a place in her unconscious where they can lie dormant without causing any damage. She doesn't intend to ever let them out. Psychiatrists and their patients might be of the opinion that it is better to process things, but what is wrong with repression? Until now she's managed really well to clamp everything down in her unconscious. She assumes there's a good reason why her mind should be capable of doing this.

'Mummy,' Anouk says with difficulty. 'I'm so thirsty.'

Lisa is thirsty too. Her tongue lies in her mouth, dried up and heavy; her saliva is thick and syrupy. It tastes awful.

He's leaving us here to starve and die of thirst, she thinks. Two very simple murders: he doesn't even have to get his hands dirty.

The images that Lisa has managed to repress return in full force. She once saw a television programme about a man who set fire to his own house, killing himself, his wife and their children.

It's difficult to get inside the mind of a child killer, the psychiatrist had concluded on the programme. Researchers don't have much to go on other than motive: in half of the cases the parents turn out to have been in serious trouble. Suicide and killing their children to prevent the whole family from having a miserable life is for many the only way out. Everyone has a space where he or she saves up revenge, hatred and jealousy, the psychiatrist had explained. But normal people clear it out now and again, so that the space doesn't become overcrowded.

The day slips by. The darkness and gloom act as a sedative. Her struggle against thirst turns into resignation. She feels the black hole beneath her, tugging her down. The temptation to just let herself sink is great. She hasn't slept properly for ages. Stumbling into the darkness and resting feels nice. Nothing else to think about. No one can harm her. She closes her eyes and thinks of Mark.

When a loud noise startles her, she has no idea how long she has been out. Anouk is lying next to her with her eyes closed, breathing deeply and regularly. Lisa lifts her arm up with some difficulty and looks at her watch. Almost seven: it's evening again.

She listens, tense, but the house has fallen silent again.

Her head feels heavy, her body weak. She can hardly see a thing: just a narrow strip of light under the door at the top of the stairs. The spectre of thirst pokes up its head again. Her tongue, glued to the roof of her mouth, feels like a piece of dead meat.

She tries to concentrate on the sound that woke her up. It sounded like a door slamming shut. Has Kreuger left?

She attempts to get up, but an attack of dizziness makes her fall back on to the cushions. She gathers herself and slowly rises again. She stands up carefully and shuffles towards the stairs. She works herself up them, one at the time, her forehead clammy. Despite her shaking hands, she manages to get the key in the lock. She waits for a while and then rests her ear against the door. She can hear voices in the sitting room. One of them is very familiar. Mark?

Hope flaps in her chest like a freed bird.

Lisa turns the key and hesitates for a few seconds. Then, checking that Anouk is still sleeping, she carefully pushes at the door.

Holding her breath, she opens it enough to squeeze through. She is desperate to drink. She takes a step into the utility room. Kreuger's voice is suddenly so loud that it sounds like he's standing next to her. Lisa reflexively jumps back.

It's a few seconds before she's fully convinced that she's still alone.

Her eyes longingly roam around the utility room.

There are only bottles of wine in the rack. The big packs of soft drinks are in the garage, but she'll never make it that far. She'll have to rely on the kitchen.

She inches towards the kitchen and listens, but only Kreuger is talking. Meanwhile, she keeps her eyes focused on the worktop, on the shining taps. One for hot and one for cold. She only has to turn them for a life-saving stream to flow. She can already feel the freshness of the water in her dehydrated mouth, feel how the liquid will rinse the mucus from her tongue and down her throat. Whoever is in there can wait a few seconds.

Her eyes glued to the taps, she shuffles to the worktop and puts her mouth under them.

The fresh stream rushes inside, and she drinks and drinks, without getting enough. Kreuger's voice breaks through again, interrupted by another that seems rather stern. It sounds like Mark's voice. Lisa straightens up and listens. My God, it is Mark. Should she call for help – can she take that risk? But before she can make a decision, she hears a scream in the sitting room, followed by loud moans.

She tiptoes towards the kitchen door. And carefully peers around the corner into the sitting room.

40

Kreuger is leaning forward with his back to Lisa. Mark is in the same position but Lisa recognises him at once. That long, straight back, dark hair, slightly too long neck, hands balled into fists betraying fear as well as anger. Mark is taller than Kreuger, but the long, razor-sharp knife that Kreuger is holding to his throat renders him totally helpless. He's not in a position to speak. Only Kreuger's voice is audible, soft and hissing.

'So you're the bastard who cheated on his wife with this slut here?'

'Don't do it,' she hears Mark beg. 'Please.'

His plea takes a while to enter Lisa's stupefied brain. She looks around feverishly. A knife, any weapon, it doesn't matter what. If she waits any longer that lunatic will do something with the knife.

'Trap shut, prick. I was talking,' Kreuger snarls.

He begins to talk about being faithful and people not being capable of it any more. Lisa doesn't wait.

There aren't any knives. There is only the chair at the kitchen table. Lisa turns around and grabs hold of the chair's back.

The kitchen isn't big, but suddenly the distance that Lisa, the chair clamped in her hands, has to cross is enormous. It is curious how heavy such an unimposing wooden chair can be. Her heart races, and there seems to be so little oxygen in her lungs that she wonders whether she'll make it as far as Kreuger. Breathing is hard and she pants; any second now he'll hear her. She realises that she's hyperventilating. But she has no choice: she has to attack Kreuger with the chair, even if it means that he'll kill Mark and then her.

The open doorway is like a portal into unknown, dangerous territory. Just as Lisa is about to announce her presence, Kreuger draws the knife across Mark's throat. Mark falls to the side, his face towards Lisa. It takes a second before the blood begins to flow, as though his body hasn't quite understood what's happened to it. At first just a trickle seeps from the wound, but then the levees burst. As though that's not enough, Kreuger begins to stab at Mark's body with terrifying fervour, getting rid of all of his frustrations in one fell swoop.

Lisa races back and grabs hold of the doorpost. Something in her spills over, coating her body in ice, making each heartbeat reverberate around her head. In a split second, her field of vision is reduced to the section of floor where Mark is lying. He can see her. Not totally conscious, yet aware he's going to die, he keeps his eyes fixed on hers.

I love you, they say. *Even though I've made mistakes, I've always loved you.*

I know and I've never stopped hoping you'd come to me.

I'm so sorry. I'm so terribly sorry.

His eyes become glassy.

Stay with me, Lisa begs.

She tries to focus on him, but he drifts away from her in a fog of tears. Her most powerful thoughts aren't enough to keep him with her, and she knows this is the end. The awareness that any hope of reunion has been sliced away by the stroke of a knife is replaced by the realisation that nothing will ever fill her with such strong feelings again. Simply because she wouldn't be able to bear it – the intense pain that races through her now is just too great.

Mark draws three more rasping breaths, and with each gulp of air more and more of Lisa's nerve endings seem to die, until she is completely numb.

Mark stares ahead with vacant eyes. Eyes that had admired her, eyes that had winked at her, and cried when she broke off their relationship. Eyes that never stopped looking at her, full of love. Eyes that gave her hope, despite everything else.

Lisa clings to the doorpost and uses every last resource to keep her grief inside. She sees Kreuger stand up, about to turn around. She takes a step backwards, but the chair is still in the doorway.

His footsteps set off a flight reflex. Her body is so weak and powerless that she doesn't stand a chance in a fight with him. She is condemned to die if she goes back into the basement, but she must. Anouk is there.

The basement door is still open. Lisa runs. Just as Kreuger enters the kitchen, she turns the key in the lock and stays dead still.

Kreuger's heaving breathing is clearly audible on the other side of the door. She doesn't move a muscle. Although it feels like she's been standing there endlessly, it's only a few minutes before Kreuger leaves the utility room. She listens to his footsteps. Then she hears him rummaging around in the garage. After a while she hears a thud against the door. For a second she thinks the door will burst open. But then she realises that he is nailing it shut. Wooden planks are slapped up, nails force their way in, the whole house reverberates with the hammering. Anouk lies still on the ground and doesn't react to any of it.

Lisa sinks to her knees at the top of the stairs and cries with her face against the door.

41

Senta drives slowly. She studies every house that looms up on her left, but each time she knows straightaway it's not the one she's looking for.

And then, to her amazement, she sees it. It's below the embankment, surrounded by fields. This is the house in her head; she recognises it at once. She was here before she had the accident; it's the only possible explanation.

Senta turns off the embankment and drives down a narrow track to the bottom. She stops her car where the road forks, parks as tight to the verge as possible and gets out.

Nothing moves in or around the house. Looks like she's unlucky and nobody's home.

She walks between the dwarf box hedges and along the gravel path to the front door. An old-fashioned-sounding ring fills the hall when she presses the bell.

There's no reply. She presses again and holds her ear to the door, but when the ringing has died away there's still no sound.

To the right of the house there's an extension with a garage door. If she really wants to check that nobody's home, she'll have to walk around the house. That's going a bit far.

On the other hand, what if the people who live here are busy in the garden and haven't heard her?

Senta hesitates for a while, then walks around to the back of the house. A large terrace stretches out in front of her, surrounded by borders full of hydrangeas, phlox, hollyhocks and salvias. Behind them the blades of a windmill slowly revolve. There are a few sheets and a nightdress on the washing line. A sheet has fallen on to the grass, and the contents of the peg basket are strewn about.

It feels like she's experienced this before. She looks at the pegs and shakes her head in confusion. Then she goes on to the terrace and starts: there's a man at the window. His arms are crossed, and his gaze is focused right on her. It's as though he's been keeping an eye on her the whole time.

Intuitively she takes a step backwards, but then the tension is broken by his smile.

Senta returns his smile hesitantly. The man

disappears, reappears in the kitchen and unlocks the door.

'Good afternoon,' he says with a friendly face, full of expectation.

'Good afternoon. Excuse me for bothering you. I'm sorry if it seems cheeky to have gone round the back, but I wanted to ask you something. It's important.'

The man raises his eyebrows and waits, as though she might be able to explain what's so important in a couple of words. But she doesn't have much choice if he's not going to invite her in.

'I was here a few days ago,' she begins. 'On Monday afternoon. It was very misty.'

'Yes,' the man says slowly.

'I got lost,' Senta continues, 'and I think I came here to ask for directions. Do you remember seeing me?'

A frown joins his eyebrows together. 'Monday afternoon?'

'Maybe there wasn't anyone home when I called. I can't remember anything myself, you see. Just after that I had a serious accident. I drove into the water a little further up the road.' She nods vaguely at the embankment, and the man looks at her with a little more interest.

'I read about it in the paper,' he says. 'Was that you?'

'Yes, but I've lost my memory of what happened before the accident. But I keep seeing this house in my mind's eye. That's why I thought—'

'Come in for a while.' He holds open the door invitingly, and Senta enters gratefully. There's an intense smell in the kitchen.

'How kind of you to spare me the time. It's important that I start to fill in that missing hour, you see. There's so much I don't understand . . .'

He smiles and offers her his hand. 'I'm Mark.'

Senta squeezes his hand. 'Senta.'

Mark precedes her into the sitting room and gestures at the sofa. 'Take a seat, Senta.'

It sounds more like an order than a friendly invitation, but Senta isn't bothered by this. Some people are gruff, and she's just happy she'll get the chance to find out more.

She sits down. The blinds have been lowered against the setting sun, and the room is bathed in a soft, orange light.

'So you don't remember me,' she says.

'No, I wasn't here on Monday. If you spoke to anyone, it would have been my wife,' he says as he sits down too.

'Oh, yes, that's possible, of course.'

'I'll ask her when she gets home. Or I'll phone her. I can see it's important to you.' He leans forward slightly, his arms on his knees. 'But you don't have a single memory of that day?'

'Of that day I do, but not of the hour running up to the accident. I don't understand what I was doing around here or why I was driving so stupidly fast that I went over the bank. The only thing I can remember is this house. So I decided to return to the scene of the accident and look for the house. That's why I'm here.'

Mark nods slowly. 'I understand. Do you know what – I'll just go and give my wife a call. Do you have a moment?'

To Senta's surprise he goes into the kitchen and closes the door behind him. Another door opens and closes, and then there's a sound of thumping somewhere further away. In the garage?

Senta wrinkles her nose a couple of times. The strange smell is in here too.

She gets up and wanders around the room. What a lovely big house this is. Nicely decorated too, just her taste. She carefully studies the photographs on the dresser. Lots of shots of a small, dark-haired little girl, mostly together with an attractive blonde woman and a man with shoulder-length dark hair.

A door opens and closes in the kitchen, and Senta quickly sits back down on the sofa. Mark comes in and gives her an apologetic smile. 'I was doing some DIY in the garage and left my mobile there. I've called her, but my wife isn't answering.'

'Oh,' Senta says disappointedly.

'I'll get her to give you a ring, all right?'

His tone has suddenly changed, as though he can't quite keep up the polite way they've been talking to each other. Something about his bearing – the tight line around his mouth and the tense way he is standing – tells Senta that for one reason or another he's doing his best to appear friendly.

Maybe she'd better leave. Just a quick trip to the loo first – she's got a long journey back. She asks for permission with an apologetic smile, and Mark acquiesces with a curt nod.

As she's sitting on the toilet, Senta looks around her. Even this space has been made cosy. On the shelf above the toilet there are scented candles and soaps and even a handmade calendar on the wall, complete with pictures. Senta can't resist the temptation to turn the pages. On each one is a hand-written line saying where the picture was taken and who it shows.

Crete. Mark, Anouk and Lisa.

Senta looks in shock at the photo. She recognises the woman from the pictures on the dresser. She also sees a toddler and a handsome man with longish dark hair, but that isn't the Mark who is walking around this house. How strange. And the man is acting so oddly. Something's wrong. She doesn't know what or why, but something is wrong in this house. And at that moment she remembers why the man looks so familiar. She's seen him before, on the news – his name is Kreuger, something Kreuger.

Oh my God! She has to get away quickly!

She hurries to get up, pulls up her pants and brushes her skirt down over her knees. She's about to unlock the door when she hears Mark, or Kreuger, or whatever he's called, coming into the hall. Senta pulls back her hand as though the lock is electrified. Her heart is in her throat. She throws a soap into the toilet bowl, followed by a second shortly afterwards. The splashing sounds, following by the noise of the toilet roll uncoiling, make Mark return to the sitting room.

Senta quickly shoots the lock and opens the door. Through a chink in the open sitting-room door she can see Mark staring out of the window, his hands in his trouser pockets. She rushes to the front door and pushes down on the handle. It doesn't give; the door is locked.

42

The panic attack courses through Senta, gripping like a tight band around her chest and sweeping a layer of sweat across her forehead. She pants and wheezes. She tries to speak sternly to herself to prevent herself from hyperventilating.

Calm down, calm down, she thinks. Don't let him see that you've sussed him. If you deal with this in the right way, you'll be able to walk straight out of here.

At the same time, she asks herself how she can return to the sitting room. He'll see in a single glance what kind of a state she's in. But she can't stay here either.

While Senta is pulling herself together, the sitting-room door swings open, and she is shocked to find Kreuger standing there before her.

She is struck by how effortlessly his name had

popped out of her memory. She hadn't paid that much attention to the news story about his being missing. If she had, she'd know what kind of man she's dealing with now.

She rubs her hands on her skirt and looks at Kreuger's inquisitive face.

'Everything all right?' he asks.

Senta smiles weakily. 'Low insulin levels. I should have eaten something before I left the house. I missed lunch and after a while things start to go wrong.'

It's not clear whether he believes her, but he looks at her carefully.

'I really should go, I'm holding you up.' Her voice sounds uncertain. To hide her fear she turns back to the front door and tugs at the handle. 'Oh, it's locked,' she says fakely. 'Never mind, I'll go back out the way I came in. I'll find it.'

Kreuger leans against the doorpost and smiles. It's an odd way of seeing someone out. A voice in Senta's head screams at her to get out quickly, no time for procrastination. She steps past Kreuger, and their bodies brush briefly. Then she's in the sitting room and has to restrain herself from running.

Just do it, she impresses on herself. Just say goodbye normally; otherwise he'll get suspicious.

Her heels click on the wooden floor on the way to the kitchen. Halfway there she turns around and says over her shoulder, 'Thanks for your time. It would be great if your wife could call me.'

At the same time she realises she hasn't given him her telephone number, but she pretends not to notice this. Kreuger doesn't say anything. He stands in the same position, leaning against the doorpost, just watching her broodingly.

Alarm bells ring in her head. She dashes into the kitchen and throws herself at the back door.

It's locked. Panic really hits her then and she begins to scream, to push and pull. She swings the chair next to the kitchen table against the door, but it doesn't budge.

It's too late now, she sees, because Kreuger is with her and has something in his hands that makes her wild with fear.

In a desperate attempt to defend herself, she brings the chair down on Kreuger, but he brushes away the attack with a single stroke of his hand. Then he grabs the chair from her hands and tosses it to one side.

An electricity cable hangs in his hand. Senta's brain refuses to work, completely paralysed, but her instinct for self-preservation is harder to switch off.

Her muscles in her neck and shoulders tighten, like those of a cornered cat. A primitive urge breaks free in her and turns her fear into rage.

She throws herself at Kreuger with a scream.

Surprised by her attack, he falls back against the worktop. For a moment he is powerless against the violence of her clawing fingers, scratching nails and rising knee, which pounds into his crotch. Swearing loudly, he sinks down to the ground.

Senta runs into the sitting room. Her eyes dart around. The doors are locked, so the only place where she can run is upstairs. But she has no idea whether she can get out there, and there's a serious chance she'll be trapped. She'll have to find a weapon.

The first within hand's reach is a lamp with a cast iron base. A few seconds later it flies through the window, breaking the glass with a deafening crash. Using another, identical lamp, Senta knocks away as many of the glass shards obstructing her exit as she can.

Kreuger staggers into the room, and she screams. She holds the lamp base in front of her like a weapon, but this time Kreuger doesn't let her surprise him. When she raises the lamp to hit him, he grabs her arm and turns it ninety degrees.

Senta drops the lamp with a cry of pain, and the next instant she feels the cable around her neck. Her hand goes to her throat automatically in an attempt to pull away the noose, but Kreuger just pulls tighter. She is powerless. All she can do is let out a few strangled sounds. Kreuger takes a couple of steps backwards, forcing her to walk backwards too, almost hanging herself.

'Did you really think you'd get out of here alive?' Kreuger snaps at her. 'I wanted to do it quickly and painlessly, but perhaps I should take my time.'

The pressure and pain are almost unbearable. Senta's eyes bulge, shockwaves pulse through her body, and flashes of light shoot through her field of vision.

She has felt like this before and said farewell to life. The memory of that feeling suddenly comes back to her in a flash. If she'd had a LifeHammer it would never have come to that. She would have been able to smash the window and swim away from her car.

Bright colours and strange forms appear behind her eyelids, among them a LifeHammer picked out in blazing fluorescent yellow.

One of her hands continues its hopeless attempt to get the electricity cable from her neck; the other feels for her coat pocket and reaches into it. A tapered, very sharp weapon pricks her palm. Somehow she gets it out, swings it forward and then back, using all her strength to smash it between Kreuger's legs.

A direct hit was inevitable, and Kreuger's high

screech is no surprise. The cable around her neck loosens a fraction, and she quickly seizes the chance to worm her fingers under it. Before Kreuger can react, she swings the hammer again, this time upwards. It strikes home in his face.

Freed from the pressure around her neck, Senta stumbles forward, into the sitting room. She sees Kreuger panting. He reaches for his eye with an almost childish sob.

Senta snorts like an animal fighting for its life, the hammer poised for attack, sweat prickling in her eyes.

But Kreuger has something else on his mind. He sinks sobbing and cursing on to his knees, his hands pressed against one of his eyes. Blood drips through his fingers.

Her sons' excited cheers fill Senta's head, the wild cries that accompany the violent video games they so love playing. Finish him off! Kill him!

A few seconds ago she had acted in self-defence. But to go over to a wounded man and deliberately finish him off is beyond her.

Half crying, she gets out her mobile phone and dials 112. As Kreuger crawls across the floor, screaming with pain, she explains as well as she can what has happened and where she is.

'We are on our way, madam,' the call handler says. Out of the corner of her eye, Senta sees Kreuger edging his way towards her. She lifts up her weapon in a flash.

'Stay away from me or I'll smash your brains out!' she screams. 'I've called the police. They're on their way!'

Kreuger slowly gets up, one hand still covering his eye. 'Filthy bitch, did you really think you'd live to tell this story. I'll . . .' He launches himself at her, but his coordination is off. A quick step to one side is enough to avoid him, and Kreuger hits his head against the open kitchen door.

The impact is so hard that for a moment Senta thinks he's broken his neck. She looks at him warily from a few steps away. Even lying still on his back, his eyes closed, she doesn't trust him one inch. She walks around him in a semicircle, studying him from all angles, but doesn't take a single step in his direction. Her body is shaking so heavily that the LifeHammer moves backwards and forwards in her hand.

What she needs to do is stand here and keep an eye on him. If he moves, she can hit him again. The police are coming; it will take about ten minutes, a quarter of an hour at the most. Then this nightmare will be over. She can manage that.

The next instant she hears something. Senta pricks up her ears. There's a banging noise some-where in the house. Again and again she hears it.

Senta looks around, not understanding. Is there someone else here?

Her eyes glide to the photograph of the woman and girl on the dresser, and suddenly she knows why she had to return to this house.

43

After casting one last glance at Kreuger, who is lying motionlessly on the floor, Senta goes into the kitchen. She inspects everything around her, but it all seems normal. But she hears someone crying for help. It sounds muffled, as though they might be in a cupboard, but it is most probably coming from behind the door in the utility room, which has been battened shut. Either in a great hurry or a great rage, someone has haphazardly nailed five planks across the door. It's not hard to guess whose work this is. There are a couple of empty bottles of methylated spirits lying in the corner. The planks barring the door are drenched in it, and there's a big puddle on the floor. It's not hard to guess what he was planning to do.

Pressing her face to the door, Senta shouts, 'Is anybody there?'

'Yes! We're trapped in here! Help us!' a female voice shouts back.

She'll need tools to get the planks off.

'The door has been battened shut. I'm looking for something to open it with,' she shouts.

'The other door leads to the garage.' The trapped woman's voice sounds closer now. She's probably standing just on the other side of the door.

Senta looks at the garage door and sees that it's ajar. As soon as she opens it, a strong smell seeps out, a smell of iron that has penetrated the whole room. At the same time she sees a dark shape lying on the ground.

Her first impulse is to dart back and slam the door shut. Instead she screws up her courage, turns on the light and glances at the shape: it's a man wrapped in a blood-soaked rug. It doesn't take much to ascertain that he is no longer alive. He is lying on his stomach, but a wide trail of blood leading from the door to the body makes it clear what has taken place in the house.

Someone has mopped up the blood in the house, but left the garage as it is.

Senta averts her gaze, walks past the body and looks for tools on the workbench. Plenty of choice. She returns to the utility room with a crowbar. She puts the claw behind the first plank determinedly. She places one foot against the wall and pulls hard.

It's slow going and costs her more energy than she'd expected, but after a while the planks lie in a pile at her feet.

'The planks have gone, but I don't have the key,' Senta calls out.

By way of response, a key grates in the lock on the other side of the door, and it opens cautiously.

A pale female face, framed with messy blonde hair, peers at her through the narrow opening. 'Where is he?' she whispers.

Senta nods in the direction of the sitting room. 'He's there. Lying on the floor unconscious. Or dead, I'm not sure. Come.'

She slowly reaches out a hand for the woman and gently forces her to come out.

Senta is overcome with a feeling of sympathy. What on earth has this poor woman been through?

'I'm Senta,' she says softly. 'Don't be afraid. It's over. He can't hurt you any more.'

Tears appear in the woman's eyes. 'Really?' she whispers. 'Has he gone?' Then recognition crosses her face. 'You're the woman who was at the window, who went to get help. Right?'

Senta slowly nods. That must be what happened, even though she can't remember.

'Do you live here? Are you Lisa?'

Lisa nods.

The two woman look at each other for a time, and then Lisa turns around and goes back down the stairs. She returns with a little girl in her arms and lays her on the kitchen floor. The child opens her eyes and begins to mutter incomprehensibly.

Senta rushes forward. 'My God!'

'Water,' is all Lisa says.

Senta needs no more explanation than this. She fills a glass, sees straws on the table against the wall and puts one in the water. As Senta helps the girl get up, Lisa holds the glass of water out to her. Only once the first few sips have gone down her throat can the girl focus on drinking.

'So, is that better?' Senta asks gently; and, looking at Lisa, she says, 'She's dehydrated; she needs to go to hospital.'

'Where's Kreuger?' Lisa asks again.

She gets up suddenly and goes to the doorway that leads to the sitting room. Without saying a word she looks at Kreuger's motionless body on the floor and the wound to his eye. 'He's not dead,' she says flatly.

Senta has followed her and lays a hand on Lisa's arm. 'He can't hurt us any more; he's badly wounded. I've called the police. Listen, they're coming.'

She holds a finger in the air to point out the distant sound of sirens.

'He's still alive.' Lisa bends over Kreuger's body warily.

'Mummy . . .' Anouk says fearfully.

Senta pulls the girl back. 'He can't do anything to you any more, sweetheart.'

But Kreuger suddenly groans. He tries to sit up and then sees Lisa. He reaches out for her with a ferocious snarl.

Lisa jumps back screaming, just out of his reach. She lunges for the crowbar Senta used to free them and pulls it towards her.

Meanwhile, Kreuger is reeling towards them, one hand pressed to his eye.

Lisa relives the moment when he broke into the house and smashed her to the ground. She relives every terrifying moment of the past week. She sees his reddened face as he rapes her in her own bed, and in her thoughts she is vomiting into the toilet bowl again.

Finally she thinks of Mark. Of the love in his eyes before the light went out in them.

Lisa feels it coming. The rage that she has had to repress for so long builds up, faster and faster, looking for an exit. Revenge builds up in her, fighting to emerge. Her anger is now too powerful an emotion to hold back. It shoots out from her like a geyser.

She takes a step towards Kreuger and his

expression changes. He recoils as she raises the crowbar with both hands.

He stumbles and falls to the floor. Something like pleading appears in his eyes, but Lisa sees only the derision, tyranny and threat that had contorted his face previously.

'Your day-release is over,' she says. The pain in her hand has miraculously disappeared, and she brings the crowbar down on him with all her strength.

'It's finished, finished, finished!'

When Kreuger has stopped moving, and the floor and her clothes are stained with blood, she lets the crowbar drop limply from her hands.

'Come here. Sit down.' Shocked, Senta wraps her arm around Lisa and leads her to the sofa, where Lisa continues to sob soundlessly. She helps Anouk up on to the sofa next to her mother and forces herself to walk back to Kreuger's mutilated body. She has to spend much longer than she'd like rummaging in his pockets for the front-door key. Her hands are covered in blood when she goes into the hall. It seems like hours ago that she'd stood at the door, ringing the bell in vain. She turns the key with shaking hands and opens the door wide.

Then she returns to Lisa and Anouk and sits down next to them on the sofa. They don't say a word; they just listen to the police sirens in the distance. The three of them wait there together until the wailing sound finally stops in front of the door.

CHANNELLING GREAT CONTENT FOR YOU TO WATCH, LISTEN TO AND READ.

canongate.tv

   Follow us